Mending the...

**DeeAnna
Galbraith**

Jewel in the
Garden

Darcy Carson

Long Distance
Romance

Pam Binder

A Collection of Sweet and Sensual
Spring Romances
written by
Pam Binder
Darcy Carson
DeeAnna Galbraith

Edited, arranged, and published by
Reads Publishing

Contact information: Pam Binder, pambinder.com, Darcy Carson, darcycarsonbooks.com, and DeeAnna Galbraith, deeannagalbraith.com

Cover art by Angela Carson

Print ISBN: 978-1-7350188-4-3
Digital ISBN: 978-1-7350188-5-0

Mending the Past

DeeAnna Galbraith

DEDICATION

For my brother, Jim Crittenden, a roper and cowboy poet. Thanks for all your help, bro.

CHAPTER ONE

Trey Killian walked out of the Northern Nevada Correctional Center; his three-year sentence finished.

He'd written to the last address he had for his half-brother, Jace, a P.O. Box in Phoenix, telling him when he was getting out. Since Jace was a rodeo bum, always looking for another poker game Trey held no hope he would be here waiting.

Shrugging deeper into his faux sheepskin jeans jacket, Trey scanned the snow-covered Sierra Nevada range that filled the horizon. A warmer than usual early spring had resulted in bare rock on the bench, but snow that would stay put farther up. He squinted into the cold, bright, morning sun beneath the slice of shadow his Stetson provided and started walking.

He loved being outdoors. He didn't even mind the cars ripping by. It gave him time to reflect on what he had just left and what he had in mind for his next steps. He was good with his hands and spent what free time he'd had in prison hitching horsehair; braiding horsetail hair into key fobs, watch fobs, lanyards and belts. He patted his coat pocket. His prison job and sales from his "braiding hobby," had paid pretty good. He carried a little over $2,000 in cash.

Now he could put a plan into action. Getting his horse back.

At the start of his third year, Trey had asked to be on the list of inmates who had the opportunity to train a wild mustang. The federal government program used teams to thin out the mustang population and sent some of them to the correctional center in Nevada to be broken into sellable horses. Trey missed being around horses and sold himself hard as a man with experience. The prison administration knew, however, that he was convicted of overdosing a horse that had died. He hadn't, but never told them different. His experience won them over as they were short-handed and decided to give him a chance. A chance based on strict supervision during his training sessions. He agreed and was assigned a crazy four-year-old mare named Duster. Even now, six months later, he wasn't sure if he'd trained sanity into her, or she had saved his.

He wanted Duster back.

Not an easy goal, but one that was prompted when he'd overheard a prison office aide talking to another trainer about Duster being lucky enough to be going to a woman in

Wickenburg Arizona to be trained as a roping horse. Wickenburg, a town that claimed to be the roping capital of the world. Trey was at his best roping and if Wickenburg obliged, he might be able to polish his skills and get enough money to make an offer for Duster.

He set his jaw. She had to sell Duster to him. He knew he didn't have enough money to buy the mare outright, but maybe he could negotiate a payment plan, or work off the price on the woman's ranch. The rest of his plan, still a little vague, as to where he would go without someplace to stable Duster and bunk down, himself.

Getting to the little town was his next move. Or actually next after he found a decent Mexican restaurant and a clean, quiet, cheap, motel for the night. And warm. He turned up the collar on his jacket. The motel needed to be warm.

He heard it before it came up on him. A seriously aged pickup, with a grinding gear shift, pulled onto the shoulder in front of him. He hadn't even stuck out his thumb. That was weird. Trey approached as the passenger window squeaked and clattered down. He peered inside, expecting . . . Well, not expecting who he saw. An elderly Mexican woman dressed in a cowboy shirt and jeans, with silver braids wrapped on the top of her head. She smiled with perfect teeth. "Want a ride into town?"

Trey blinked. "Um, that would be great."

She nodded. "Cost ya."

Stranger and stranger. "Sorry, I'm low on funds right now."

The woman nodded. "Information, son. That's all I want. Get in."

The wind chill factor persuaded him. He yanked hard on the door that squeaked in protest as he opened it and climbed in.

She hit her blinker and pulled back into traffic. "Did you know Hector Alvarez?"

He'd known a Hector Alvarez from working a recent stint in the prison kitchen, but what was he to her? Before he could ask, she threw another smile. "My grandson. Did something stupid and got sent to the center. Too proud to let anyone visit him. So, this is how I get my scoop on how he's doing." She tipped her head. "Most guys just out take the bus, but you're different. You do something stupid too?"

Trey laughed out loud. Yeah, he had. "Your grandson have a tattoo of the Virgin Mary on his upper right shoulder?"

She nodded. "That's him. How's he doing?"

Trey couldn't resist. "He's keeping clean. Last time I saw him, he was in the kitchen, up to his elbows in hot, soapy water."

Her cackle filled the truck's cab. "Just for that, I'll take you anywhere you want to go in Carson City."

"Thanks. Know of a cheap motel with a good Mexican restaurant within walking distance?"

"I sure do. I'd invite you home and cook for you, but that's not practical right now. Next time you're in town, look up Alvarez Fruit and come visit."

Trey wondered how she knew he was leaving town. He'd also wondered why the truck's cab smelled like cherries. "Thanks."

He looked out the window. She was a good driver, and hadn't hesitated picking him up. Stopping for ex-cons just having been released was gutsy. But he noticed she drove with one hand on the wheel. Since Nevada was an open carry state, she struck him as a woman who might be smart enough to have protection in the driver door's pocket. Trey smiled. He hoped that was the case. Relaxing, he took in the sites. Although he hadn't been a resident of Carson City when he went to jail, he figured not much had changed in the last three years.

The woman pulled into the parking lot of a national motel chain. "A block west and one more block north and you'll find a reasonably-priced Mexican restaurant. Tell them Rita sent you and they'll serve the good stuff."

Hector Alvarez was one lucky guy, if his grandmother was any indication of his family dynamic, Trey thought. He took a ten from his pocket. "Can I help with the gas?"

"Thanks for the offer, but I was coming to this area of town anyway. Nice to meet you."

Trey gave the door a good, sturdy slam to make sure it would hold, and waved as the woman drove off.

The older man behind the check-in counter handed him a form to fill out and Trey did, but the guy handed it back. "You forgot to fill in your car information and license plate."

He had seen Trey get out of the pickup and knew he didn't arrive in a car, but Trey shrugged. "Don't own a car. I was going to ask your help in finding the nearest rental agency tomorrow."

The man paused. "You a friend of Rita's?"

Not knowing if that was a good thing or a bad thing, Trey gave him a non-answer. "She invited me over for dinner."

The desk attendant smiled. "Oh. Well, if she didn't shoot you, you must be okay."

Trey's room was warm and after a big, delicious lunch at the recommended restaurant, he brought the leftovers back to his room to heat up for dinner. He'd asked for a quiet room and after three years of shouts, snoring, and general nighttime prison noise, it was quiet to the point of eerie.

The next morning, Trey slept in, took a long hot shower, then stretched out and watched the news. Solitude was going to take getting used to.

The same front desk guy handed him a brochure when he checked out. "Best deal in town for car rentals is about six blocks south."

Trey rounded up the charge on his bill and paid in cash. "Appreciate it."

****

The guy at the motel was right. Trey's driver's license was still valid, but he'd never had to rent a car and was surprised when he was told cash wasn't accepted. He needed a major credit card or debit card attached to a checking account. Across the street was a small branch of a national chain bank. He wasn't about to hitch to Arizona or take a bus. Trey sighed and signed up, putting in just enough cash to cover the rental via a new debit card. His new plastic enabled him to rent a cheap sub-compact. He left the rental agency by mid-afternoon. If he made a couple of pitstops, he could be in Wickenburg in about ten hours. Driving straight through would save him one night's charge in a motel anyway. He had no job and no place to stay in the little town, but he'd work on that when he got there.

CHAPTER TWO

Eden Burris kissed her horse, Duster, on the nose. "Hey, girl. We have a new rider today. She's a little afraid of horses, so be extra gentle."

The horse bobbed her head and snorted softly.

Eden hugged her neck. "I knew I could count on you. And after she leaves, we'll go for a ride, then practice our roping. I have to come up in the ratings for better prize money and we're just the girls to do it."

Eden heard the purr of her father's electric wheelchair and turned around.

Chap Burris smiled. "You have longer conversations with that horse than you do with me."

"She *listens*," Eden shot back.

Her father spread a hand over his heart. "I'm wounded. But that not listening thing runs in the family.

Didn't I beg you not to schedule Cynthia Worden for a ride? Yet, there she is, due at ten. She's a widow too. She let me know that right out of the gate."

Eden shook a finger at him. "You know she's on the board of Desert Peace Retirement Center. Her word will go a long way in encouraging new retirees to come out here for rides. You know we can use the income."

Chap Burris pulled his lips in and grimaced. "Partly due to a certain jerk. By the way, why are you out here? Travis should be getting Duster ready. If he's even up at this hour."

Not much got past her father and Eden was tired of responding to his mention of a certain jerk, and covering for her old high school friend. She'd given Travis Holden a job when he needed one most, hoping his poor reputation was an exaggeration. It wasn't. The first few weeks he'd worked out great, then things began to slide. Always with an excuse. Bar-hopping was his favorite sport with the occasional bar fight thrown in. They could no longer afford to let Travis's reputation color theirs. "I know Dad. He's blown his last chance, but I don't see anybody lining up for room and board and what we can pay."

Pushing his point, Chap rolled over to pat Duster on the nose, slipping her a sugar cube. "Duster don't like him either."

Eden sighed. Her mare had great instincts and danced and twitched around Travis. "I'll tell Travis tomorrow morning. That'll give me time to ask around the arena today to see if anyone is interested in taking his place. Guess the two of us will have to take on more." She gave her dad a pointed look. "And one of us will have to endure riders like Cynthia."

Chap grumbled as Duster pushed at his hand, hoping for more sugar. "She's nice enough. Just nobody could take your mom's place."

True again. Patricia Burris, or Trisha, was a one-of-a-kind wife, mom, and all-around terrific person. "Yeah, but I'm running out of excuses for some of the ladies who I know come out here on the off-chance they can chat with you. You're going to have to make an appearance occasionally."

Her dad took off his ballcap and slapped it against his lap. "I used to be able to do a lot more around here. Now, I'm just a chick magnet."

Eden raised an eyebrow. Feeling sorry for himself when he didn't want to do something put Chap in the same category as a five-year-old. "Right. Well, we all have our place in the running of the ranch, now don't we?"

Chap put his hat back on and snapped it into place. "I guess."

****

There were only two riders scheduled for the morning. Eden put Cynthia on Duster and her dad dutifully came out to say hello and encourage her. The woman, clearly charmed, said she would give her blessing to the event manager to have Eden come and talk to the Desert Peace residents.

Eden's euphoria was short-lived halfway through the second ride when Travis appeared at the gate to the corral. His clothes looked slept in, but he grinned and waved. "Hey, y'all. Good morning."

It was already noon, so Eden concentrated on the client, choosing not to vent her anger at Travis in front of him. "You're looking very western in your new cowboy hat Mr. Goodman. Pretty soon you'll be able to leave the corral and take a horse out on your own."

The client, riding Eden's other horse, a gelding with the barn name, Jack of Spades, or Jack, admitted to sitting behind a desk his whole corporate life, smiled and nodded, although he still looked far from comfortable or natural. "I just might do that, Miss Burris."

Eden dreaded another confrontation with Travis. His appearance halfway through the day, strengthened her suspicion that Travis thought he could do no wrong since no one else would take the job for essentially room and board and beer money. He was right, of course, so Eden had decided to set her sights on a kid, fresh out of high school and looking to learn a lot if not earn a lot.

Her new strategy settled on, she finished with Mr. Goodman and stabled Jack before saddling Duster and heading for the arena she favored. She put in as many training hours a day as she could in the small corral on the eight acres she and her dad owned, but she needed more room and hopefully a partner to get the intense training Duster needed if she was going to be a top-notch heel horse.

Duster had a great instinctive sense in the arena too. Quick, responsive, and practically an extension of Eden's body. If the header they were paired with was quick to rope the head of the steer, she and Duster almost always caught the heels. Roping was her passion and she meant to get to, and stay in, the top of the best roping teams out there.

Inside the arena, other locals practiced their craft. Some teams performed like a graceful ballet, others, well, their style could best be described as a mugging. She knew them all and liked them. Even the crude cowboys who insisted on calling, "hey cutie, hey blondie, whatcha doin' later?" She'd been ignoring them since she was fourteen. No guy but one, had ever captured her longing like roping.

****

Trey woke up and uttered a moan. The driver's seat in the compact he'd rented didn't give near enough leg room, let alone provide a comfortable sleeping position for his six-foot-one frame. He opened his eyes and started for an instant. No colorless walls and door. Trey rubbed his face. He'd chosen to pull off the side of the road just inside the Wickenburg city limits and spend the balance of the night in the car. Poor choice. Luckily, he wasn't rousted by the police. Unluckily, the money he'd saved by not renting a room, had to be spent on clothes. He wanted to look decent when he went to talk to this Eden Burris woman about Duster.

Trey drove slowly into town, looking for an inexpensive place to shop. His search ended when he almost passed a second-hand store. Perfect. He went in and found a couple pair of jeans his size and not too badly worn, new socks, a t-shirt blazoned with the logo of a community college in the area, and a pale blue western shirt that fit him well. Thirty-seven bucks, including a used duffle, and he was out the door. He filled the gas tank of the car and used the gas station bathroom to put the soap, shampoo, and razor he'd gotten in the motel room in Carson City, to use.

Next, was his stomach. He found the nearest fast food place for breakfast and sat by a window to eat. He liked the little town that branded itself roping capital of the world. It was certainly warmer than Carson City and the area of Nevada he'd left.

After he ate, Trey approached the girl behind the counter, glancing at her name tag. "Excuse me, Tiffany. I'm looking for an address on Powder Wash Road. The guy at the gas station told me to head in this direction. Do you know how I get there?"

Tiffany flashed her braces at him and pointed out the window. "See that busy road over there? That's Constellation. Follow it out a ways and the road you're looking for is on the left. If you get to the turnoff for the rodeo arena, you've gone too far."

Trey put on his hat and smiled. "Thank you."

He had envisioned himself approaching Eden Burris and reasonably explaining his circumstances. Then he'd offer to work off the price she wanted for Duster. He had no idea what that would be or what she'd paid. Duster wasn't a trained performance horse, so she probably just used her for ranch work. He didn't care. Only wanted the horse back. He'd worry about the details later.

All of that went out the window when he arrived at the Burris ranch.

CHAPTER THREE

Trey didn't like the scene he came on as he drove onto the Burris property. A beautiful woman wearing jeans, a lavender work shirt, and dusty gold cowboy boots was standing back from a really upset guy. She held an envelope in one hand, and the reins to Duster in the other. He didn't have to get out of the car. The clear desert air carried their voices.

"I was serious about that being your last chance. Now, take your pay and clear out."

The guy shook his head. "You don't own this place. I'll talk to Chap. He understands a man needs to let off steam every once in a while."

The girl pulled her lips in, then out. "This is harder than it needs to be. When I hired you, you said you understood the terms. I don't care what you do on your free time. Unless the consequences affect your job performance. As it has, *every day*."

They didn't seem to see Trey get out of the car, but when he did, he heard a whirring sound coming from his left. An older man in a wheelchair appeared, gave him a short nod and rolled toward the arguing couple standing inside the corral.

Travis turned toward the sound and smiled. "There you are, buddy. Your daughter thinks I've been a bad influence and wants me to leave. I told her you'd understand. Besides, who're you going to get to replace me?"

Trey couldn't believe his luck. He had an idea and started toward the corral.

Duster caught wind of him. The mare jerked the reins out of the hand of who Trey assumed was Eden Burris and ran to the top rail. She jumped up, whinnying and snorting.

Trey had missed the way she used to greet him and stepped to the rail. He patted her neck and rubbed his hand up her nose. "Hey girl. You look good."

The blonde girl turned her blue gaze on him. "Who're you and how do you know Duster?"

Trey didn't want to blurt out who he was and where he'd come from. Not everyone had Rita's view of ex-cons. And that's what he was. An ex-con. He took off his hat. "Um. A guy at the arena said you might be looking to hire. I'm out of work and thought I'd check in with you. I get along well with most horses."

He hadn't answered her question, but his timing won out.

The pretty blonde tucked the envelope in the shirt pocket of the guy named Travis and walked to the rail, placing a proprietary hand on Duster and holding out the other to him. "Eden Burris."

He took her hand. "Trey Killian."

The whirring sound came closer. "Where you from, son?" The guy he assumed was Chap asked, not bothering to address Travis's question.

Trey stuck out his hand. "Most recently, near Carson City, sir." An absolute truth, but blurry. He slipped another sugar cube to Duster under the watchful eye of her owner.

The pretty woman continued. "Why'd you pick Wickenburg?"

"Change of scenery. And I thought I'd practice my roping. Lots of events here."

She glanced at the rental plates on his car, and beyond.

"If you're looking for a horse and trailer and roping gear, I don't have a horse right now and I didn't bring anything with me. Upkeep's too expensive until I find a place I want to stay a while." That was true too. He'd hated it, but sold his last horse, Sugarpop, to help pay legal fees. His trailer and gear and other clothes and boots were stored at the little outbuilding and cabin he'd inherited from his grandfather. Built in the nineteen fifties by Murdock Killian, the buildings were run down, but sat on a horse acre.

They were the poor neighbors in a rich neighborhood in Incline Village, Nevada, near Tahoe. Trey had received a number of forwarded postcards and realtor brochures while in prison telling him they were interested in selling his "valuable" property. He wasn't, but had needed to turn over the last of his savings to a friend as a three-year advance to manage the property and pay the property taxes.

Duster whickered and pushed at his shoulder, so Trey rubbed her nose again. "Is she a roping horse?"

Eden nodded. "She's in training. I'm a heeler."

This is where a little white lie came in. "I'm a header. Injured in a fall in the Pendleton Roundup. Getting back after knee surgery takes a long time." All true, but he was totally recovered as the accident had happened five years ago.

"Could your injury interfere with ranch work?"

He shook his head, but she didn't notice, her gaze following that guy Travis's exit to a beat-up pickup. He carried an armload of personal items, dumped them in the truck's bed, then got in and slammed the door before blowing gravel all over the drive as he sped away.

"He had to know that was coming, Honey," Chap said. "He's been playing on our sympathies too long."

She sighed and turned back, her single, pale blonde braid sliding over her collarbone. "I guess. At least his bad behavior won't be linked to us."

Trey could tell from her slight frown, that she felt bad about getting rid of the guy, so he changed the subject. "All healed. What kind of work are you looking for?"

"Oh, general horse care, barn maintenance a couple of hours a day. And most days, we'll have clients from Desert Peace Retirement Center coming out for horseback lessons and rides."

He blinked. "Seniors. Coming out to ride. Does your insurance cover that?"

Eden laughed. "You should see your face. If the premiums are any indication, it does. Part of your job would be to encourage a good, safe time is had by every client. It's Chap's idea and we're just getting it off the ground."

The older man spun his chair toward the house. "And with that, I'm going back in. Got a chicken casserole to put in the oven. If you decide to stay, it'll give you an idea of the fancy grub you can look forward to."

Trey really liked Eden and her dad, but was losing faith in his plan to buy back Duster. Eden Burris had been training her as a heel horse. Even if she was willing to sell her, breaking heel horse training to change her into a head horse would be confusing and frustrating for the horse *and* him. On the other hand. If he worked here, he could be near Duster and scout around for a head horse to practice on.

He shrugged. It simply could not be worse than the food he'd eaten the last three years. "What are we talking about as far as pay and other benefits?"

She named an hourly wage that barely beat what he made in prison, but adding in room and board tipped the scales considerably. "Can I have a look around?"

She nodded. "Your quarters would be in the barn. It's not much. Double bed, small bathroom with shower, and mini-fridge and microwave. A decent swamp cooler keeps it bearable in the summer if you run it 24/7."

Duster's excited state hadn't escaped her attention, either. The horse trotted along the rail beside them, whickering and nudging his shoulder. Trey figured he'd better come clean before things went any further. He stopped walking. "Something I need to tell you before this, um, interview continues."

Eden stopped too. "I know. Duster told me."

"What?"

The blonde swung that blue laser gaze at him. "Short trip to figure it out, Mr. Killian. A. Duster was a wild mustang captured by the feds. B. She was sent to the Nevada Corrections Center to be broke by an inmate. C. After she was broke, I bought her at auction. D. She obviously knows and adores you. End of the trip. You broke her." She folded her arms. "I assume that's what you needed to tell me." She tilted her head. "Interesting that my information was supposed to be confidential, but you got it. Now that you're here. What do you want?"

He stuffed his hands in his pockets. Assuming he was offered and accepted the job, this fine-looking woman would certainly keep him on his toes "She kept me sane my last year. I was hoping if I came here, I could buy her from you by working off her price. Just happened to arrive when you were giving that Travis guy the boot. Seemed like an opportunity I couldn't pass up. Until you mentioned training her as a heel horse. I couldn't undo that and train her as a head horse. Too hard on both of us. If it helps, I do need a job and a place to stay." He shrugged. "That's about it."

Trey looked her square in the face, hoping to show sincerity. Not much thawing there.

"How long were you in? And are you on parole?"

"Three years. And no. I got out free and clear two days ago."

"So, not a murderer, woman abuser, or major felon."

Trey knew where this was going. "No. And I'd prefer not to share."

Her eyes widened. "Guess if it's done, that's not really my business." She relaxed. "Now that we're clear on your original motive, one which you will not achieve, are you still interested in the job?"

His turn to be surprised. He grinned. "Yes, thank you. It may take a while, but I need to save for a horse. Plus, I can be around Duster. She loves me."

Eden's choke turned into a laugh. "I saw. Here's the deal. We give you a month on a trial basis. If you work out, you're permanent. The operative word being work. And I think we can help you with wanting to get back into shape to ride header, but I need to make a call first."

After living in a cell for three years, Trey was more than accepting of the job duties and room and board. He even liked Chap's chicken casserole with a Mexican flair. Helping bus the lunch dishes made him a big hit too.

While he and Chap cleared the dishes, Eden stripped his bedding and brought it in. "Washer and dryer right inside the back door. They're available for your use, too. I won't be doing your bedding again as long as you're here."

Trey nodded. "Fair enough. And thanks."

Chap cleared his throat. "That rental's costing him money just sitting out there. Why don't you show him where the rental agency is and let him return it? Then give him a mini tour of Wickenburg?"

Trey shrugged. "Appreciate getting out from under the rental contract, but no need to go for a tour. I got about three hours sleep last night in the car and would like to spend some time with Duster before I turn in early."

CHAPTER FOUR

Eden had conflicting emotions about Trey Killian. She'd never hired or worked with an ex-con, but he didn't seem dangerous or shady. It confused her. Besides, he couldn't be a bad guy if he'd trained Duster. Could he? Her dad was right. Duster had good instincts and from all signs she was crazy about Trey.

He wasn't too shabby in the good looks department either. Easy on the eyes at six foot or so, light brown hair nicely trimmed, really pretty gray eyes, a flat stomach which she assumed included a rockin' six pack, and a killer smile. She reined herself in. She'd been fooled by good looks and smooth talk before.

She nodded at her dad. "We'll be gone probably less than an hour."

It was interesting that Chap too, was okay with Trey almost immediately. She had a ranch to run though, and a new enterprise to get off the ground and successful as soon as possible. She hoped Trey worked out. If he did, her only sticking point was his request that he not share the reason for his imprisonment. She could go on one of those websites that reveals a person's arrest record and why, but decided against it. She might be too trusting, but if he wanted her to know at some future point, he'd tell her.

As they started to leave, Chap spoke up. "I think Trey would be interested in meeting Jenks."

Eden laughed. "Way ahead of you, Dad." Outside, Trey looked at her expectantly. Those calm, gray eyes gave her just a second of peace. A second of knowing her happy place was of her own making and yet, she could be happier. How was that possible?

She shook the strange thought away. "Jenks Robard is our next-door neighbor. He was my header partner occasionally, but just had rotator cuff surgery and is worried about his horse getting enough exercise. I can't help. Not with the crowding on our schedule."

"Better and better," Trey grinned, tossing the car keys high in the air, spinning around, and catching them.

Eden smiled. "He'll agree to let you use his mare if I ask him. He's got a mad crush on me. He says the forty years difference in our ages doesn't bother him, so I told him it doesn't bother me, either."

She got a kick out of the expression of Trey's face. It seemed to be a combination of disbelief and hope. Maybe it was wrong to dangle room and board, a job, and a horse to ride in front of a cowboy just two days out of prison, but if he was willing to work for it, she was willing to take a chance.

The drop-off of the rental went smoothly and Trey joined her in her truck. The only thing he brought out of the rental was a sad little beat-up duffle. He dropped it in the truck bed and got in. A man she figured was what? About thirty. Should have a few more belongings. "That all the gear you got there, Killian?"

"Stupid, I know," he said. "Stowed everything I had in my cabin before they processed me in."

Eden started her truck and glanced at him before pulling out. "Why is that stupid?"

Trey chuckled and glanced out the window. "Cabin's about forty-five minutes from Carson City. I left there yesterday to come here."

She opened, then closed, then opened her mouth again. "Oh. And drove, I'm guessing ten or twelve hours to get here? Without your gear?"

"Yeah. I was in a big hurry. Somewhere in the back of my mind I must've figured it was a fool's errand and I'd fail. That's the only thing I can think of to explain it."

Eden sighed. "I'm sorry about Duster. She's one of the best horses I've ever had. You did a great job."

Those nice gray eyes again. It wasn't part of the job interview, but she kinda wanted to know. "Do you have any immediate family? You, know, in case you have to leave for a family emergency or I need to notify anyone." Well, that sounded lame.

"Got a half-brother, Jace. He's hard to track down, but I'll give you his last address. That's about it."

She got a little adrenaline boost finding out there wasn't a wife out there somewhere. Which, of course, didn't rule out a girlfriend. Okay, that was nonsense. A wife or girlfriend who hadn't been with him for three years would be here. Now. And why was she thinking about the personal relationships of a guy she'd known for about an hour?

Chap was all she had too. She felt lucky every day he'd come out of that fall off Jack a year ago with only a wheelchair to contend with. A freak accident when a truck bringing in hay backfired near the corral and spooked the normally calm horse. Lucky was not how Chap saw it, but they made the best of it.

Change of subject. "Since you don't have a car, you're welcome to use this truck for any business in town. Or, uh, personal use."

Trey nodded. "Thanks. Speaking of that, is there a drug store or one of those super centers we can drop in for a few minutes on the way back to your place? I know I said I didn't need a tour, but I do need a cheap cellphone and to pick up some shampoo, a razor, and shaving cream. That kind of stuff."

Eden figured that was reasonable considering how quickly he'd left Nevada. Besides, she could pick up some ice cream for Chap. Travis had helped himself to their refrigerator frequently, without replacing what he took, and Chap was a big rocky road fan.

****

Even though the job came with room and board, Trey had a good appetite and liked sweets. He purchased a phone, a pack each of boxers and t-shirts, snacks, and bathroom paraphernalia. At checkout, he took the ice cream from Eden's hand. "My treat."

She grinned. "You won't be that free very often with your new salary."

Trey almost said it had been a long time since he shared a treat with a pretty woman, but stopped himself and shrugged. Way too familiar a thing to say to his new boss. "Maybe not, but humor me this time."

Eden favored him with a brilliant smile. "Not going to turn down free chocolate ice cream."

He went through the checkout feeling like a normal guy on a shopping trip. It gave him a lift to be trusted by two complete strangers who knew his background. Most of it, anyway.

Soon enough they arrived at Eden's ranch, both recognizing Travis's abused pickup in the drive. He was loading the minifridge from his former room, the microwave, already in the back. Eden blocked the driveway with her truck and got out, running toward him, Trey right behind her. His instincts told him it would be a bad idea to barge in and take charge. This was Eden and Chap's place and their quarrel. He would help if asked.

Eden stood in front of Travis's driver's door. "What do you think you're doing?"

He gave a drunken snort. "Takin' this stuff. It was in my room for a half a year, so under squatter's rights, it's mine. If you'd've put out, I'd still be here."

Trey sucked in air through his teeth. This guy was his own worst enemy and just lost any chance of ever working here again. Which was good for his own prospects.

Without warning, a pop sounded and Travis let out a yowl. Chap sat at the back door to the house, a pellet rifle in his hand. "I told you, you're not taking anything. And the next time you speak about my daughter like that, it won't be a pellet in your butt." He turned to Trey. "Care to give us a hand by unloading your minifridge and microwave?"

"Glad to, sir," Trey said, and took out the microwave while Eden remained by the truck door, arms crossed, and Travis hopped around the driveway swearing and rubbing the top of his back thigh.

He hadn't been in the room that was going to be his, yet, so Trey sat the small appliance down near Chap and went back for the minifridge.

Travis flipped off Chap and yelled. "I'm going to have you arrested for attempted murder, old man."

Trey frowned. "What? I swear I saw you get between a rancher and a coyote he was taking a bead on. Just your bad luck."

Eden pointed to Trey. "That's my story too. And if you come back with that accusation against Chap, I'm going to tell your mother you stole from us."

That seemed to be the magic threat. Travis jerked on his hat and climbed into his truck without speaking. He squealed his tires again, almost taking out a small barrel cactus at the edge of the driveway.

Eden dusted off her hands and sighed. "I knew hiring him was a mistake, but his mother talked me into it. Good riddance."

"Chap nodded. "He was about useless anyway. Don't think he put in a full day all the months he worked here."

Trey picked up the minifridge. He didn't think adding to their condemnation of Travis would help. He, himself, sat on a fine balance. Ex-con on one side, and their desperation at needing a hand with experience on the other. Putting in the work would speak for him. "Point me in the direction of the spare room and I'll put this back."

Turned out two doors accessed his new room. One from outside, and one from the enclosed back porch. The first thing he noticed was the smell. Seems the former resident didn't keep the tidiest living space. Trey picked out dirty laundry and the sharp scent of old vomit as the top two.

Eden followed right behind him with the microwave and carried it to the table, plugging it in. She turned, wrinkling her nose. "Sorry it's in such bad shape. I'd hoped taking out the bedding and opening a window would help. I'd also intended to give it a good scrubbing before I hired the next hand. I have back-to-back clients shortly and I need to feed and tend to Jack, so If you can stand it for one night, I'll bring in clean bedding for you and help with some deep cleaning tomorrow."

Trey shrugged. He'd slept in worse. And the fact that she didn't just dump him in a stinky room and walk away meant something. "I'll manage. If you point out the broom and mop closet I'll be set for future clean-ups."

Eden smiled. "I don't think in all the time Travis worked here, he ever asked where any cleaning products or implements were stored. I have new respect, Trey."

"And that doesn't happen often," Chap said from the doorway. "Take it from me. By the way, I fed Jack and put the bedding in the dryer. Now can I have some ice cream?"

Eden squeaked. "Oh, the groceries!" and shot past Trey. He laughed and followed her to the truck, helping to unload the packages.

CHAPTER FIVE

It had been a long, but interesting day and Trey was tired. Not too tired to spend time with Duster, though. Once he sorted his room out, he got permission from Eden to feed, then take Duster for a walk around the smaller corral. He'd purchased some apples at the store and cut them into smaller pieces for her. He swore her eyes rolled back when he held out his palm with an apple slice on it. He had really missed this horse, but had come to the conclusion she was in the right hands with Eden and Chap.

After the second client left, Eden and he closed up for the night. On the far side of the large corral lay an eight- or ten-acre piece of land. Trey stood looking over it in the twilight when Eden walked up beside him. He could swear she smelled like desert sunshine. "Did you and Duster have a nice reunion?" she asked softly.

Nice of her to ask. "Yeah. I made a mistake, though. Now she'll want apple slices every time she sees me."

Eden laughed. "Wouldn't want to be in your boots when you show up without."

"Going to keep her guessing." He nodded toward the land he was looking over. "What do you plan to do with this part of your property?"

Eden sighed. "Wish it *was* mine, but it's not. Owned by an investor who wants more than I can afford. I'd turn it into a large practice arena, that's what I'd do."

Trey was a big believer in *what ifs*. "It could happen," was his reply. Then, "good night."

****

The open window disbursed most of the sour air during the night. Trey had forgotten how the desert air had a smell and sound of its own and concentrated on that before falling fast asleep.

The teal-blue sky before sunrise, seen through a window without bars made him grateful for everything that had happened yesterday. He rubbed his face and walked into the tiny three-quarter bathroom. The shower was three feet by three feet and the overhead spray just tall enough to accommodate him. Just like the shower in the motel, it was weird having it all to himself.

Trey put on his oldest shirt and jeans and left his feet bare, then quietly went into the back porch and got everything he needed to clean his room. A half hour later, someone knocked on his door. "Hello?"

"Come in," Trey shouted over his shoulder. Pleased at his newfound privacy.

Eden peeked in at him scrubbing his bathroom floor. "Hey, you don't have to do that. I have help in once a week to do the big stuff. I was going to have them do this room because it was so bad."

Trey stood. "The cleaner your cell, the less you got hassled. Easier to keep clean too."

Eden shrugged. "My new favorite line, and my new favorite tenant. Breakfast in fifteen minutes, okay?"

He'd forgotten his job came with room *and* board. He'd planned on instant coffee, a piece of toast and sharing an apple with Duster. "Sounds great. I can make oatmeal for a hundred if you need help."

She blinked for an instant, then laughed. A sound he was beginning to really enjoy. Duster would have to wait for her apple slices, he was about to have a real home-cooked breakfast with a pretty woman. One whose soft blonde hair piled on the top of her head today.

Trey whistled through his shave, making strange faces as he did so, ran a clean rag over his boots and tucked in his shirt before walking through the back door of the house exactly fifteen minutes later.

Eden clapped. "Didn't I tell you he'd be right on time?"

"You did," Chap said. "You also said he'd probably offer to do the dishes, but I wasn't to allow it, more's the pity, since that's my job."

"Stop grousing," she said. "If you're loading the dishwasher, you can't be made to greet and charm the new clients from Desert Peace."

"There is that," Chap replied grudgingly. "I hope you've included that in Trey's job description. The women at least, will be charmed a lot quicker with tall and good lookin' than old and crooked."

Trey lay down his fork. He hoped he'd judged Chap's temperament right. "Not if I can run faster than you."

"Don't have to run faster than me," Chap winked. "Have to run faster than *them*."

Trey laughed. "I think I can manage that."

Eden crooked her eyebrow at Chap, then Trey. "He's exaggerating. A few of the ladies have teased him and are just looking for an outing or some company. Makes him cranky when they flirt."

These two, almost total strangers, had made Trey feel at ease and welcome. He would do whatever it took to keep that feeling.

Eden stood and took her dishes to the sink. "We need to saddle Duster *and* Jack. Both of today's clients are new to us. The first one claims she has no experience on a horse, the second says he used to ride all the time, but it's been a while." She pinned Chap with a look. "Three new clients this week. I told you we should've bid on two horses at that auction. If they're all trained as well as Duster, I need to attend the next auction coming up in a couple of weeks."

Chap nodded and pulled his mouth down at one corner. "Never thought that idea would take off like it has." His gaze found Trey. "Maybe take this guy along as an expert while I hold down the fort."

Eden's eyes sparked. "Expert knowledge? Is that what you're saying? I need help picking out another horse?"

Trey was confused. As far as he could tell, she had an amazing grasp on what made a good horse. So, why was Chap saying otherwise?

Eden's father showed no remorse. "Just a suggestion. Trey knows the ins and outs of the program and the guys doing the training. He might have insight on what the auction has to offer. Besides, you told me all his personal gear is located less than an hour from where you're going. Maybe kill two birds with one stone. Besides, he could help with the driving."

****

Eden had no immediate response to her dad's logic. He made sense, but that didn't keep her from feeling like a virgin being sacrificed at the volcano's edge. This wasn't the first time he'd suggested she team up with an eligible man to get something done. And good suggestion or not, her dad was messing in her admittedly non-existent love life and she didn't like it. "That's enough, Dad. We'll talk about this later."

Trey looked everywhere but at her. "Excuse me, but I need to make a few phone calls. There are some people who should have my new number."

As soon as he left, Eden finished clearing the table without speaking to Chap. She was saved from letting her temper loose when they heard a car in the driveway. She spoke low in case Trey was within hearing distance. "We'll be busy for the next couple of hours. If your suggestion causes Trey to, oh, I don't know, leave in the middle of the night because you threw your daughter in his path, I will be extremely angry with you." With that she left in what she hoped was a huff.

Chap ducked his head, but she'd seen that before and knew it was not a real sign of repenting.

Eden put on her most genuine smile and walked out to meet their new client, a tiny woman in a new cowboy hat a shade too big for her. The western apparel shops in town must be doing a booming business. "Ms. Williams? Welcome."

The woman nodded absentmindedly, staring past Eden toward the corral where Trey was leading Duster. "Is that your husband?"

Eden glanced over her shoulder and had what could only be described as a slow-motion movie moment. Faded jeans and shirt, dusty boots, and a well-worn Stetson covered a gorgeous cowboy named Trey Killian. "Um, no. That's Trey. He works here."

The small woman grinned. "If I was thirty years younger, I'd give you a run for your money with that one. Will he be helping me today?"

Eden saw the future of her endeavor as wildly successful with Trey helping the senior ladies. "Yes, of course."

"Lovely," Ms. Williams replied, on her way toward the corral.

Trey couldn't have heard the woman, but Eden could tell he saw the client's eagerness. Heck, you could see it from the International Space Station.

Her dad's chair whirred up quietly behind her. He cleared his throat. "Sorry, Honey. I only want what's best for you, and I have a feeling that man is it. Subtlety aside, I'll stay out of your business from now on. But you gotta admit the two of you traveling together to pick up another horse and his gear was a great idea."

Eden sighed as she watched Trey touch the brim of his hat and speak to the woman he helped onto Duster. "Only as boss and employee, Dad. And only because one roundtrip for two reasons makes economic sense. And if he's still working here after that blatant attempt to throw us together."

"Okee dokee," Chap said and chuckling, returned to the house.

A half hour after Ms. Williams ride concluded, Eden got a call from Cynthia Worden. "I've talked it over with the other board members and we'd like to invite you to talk to our residents about visiting your ranch to take riding lessons. And if he's not too busy, maybe your helper, Mr. Killian I think his name is, can come along."

Subtle, Eden thought. *You're invited, but bring the hunky cowboy in case we lose interest in your talk.*

"Yes, of course we'll be there, Ms. Worden. What day and time?"

"How about this Thursday at three o'clock? We'll mark you down for an hour."

Eden sucked in a small gasp. Day after tomorrow to have a ready presentation? They'd been laying the groundwork, but she hadn't thought it would bear out so soon. "That's fine. We'll be there. And thank you for the opportunity."

She ended the call and grimaced. Dragging Trey into her dream as arm candy to tempt the ladies, made her feel dishonest. She needed to let him know what he'd be getting himself into.

Shouts of 'whoa, whoa' came from the corral. Eden hurried out to see the senior gentleman who 'used to ride all the time,' dragging on Jack's reins, his face a red mask. Trey trotted over and stepped in front of the gelding, soothing him almost immediately.

"I had Jack out earlier and he's got high spirits today. Not your fault. I learned if you loosen the reins a little and talk to him calmly, he tends to settle right down."

"I know that," the man said. "I let him have his way and those high spirits took over. I've recently recovered from hip surgery and didn't want to test my new hip too soon."

"Smart," Trey said. "A man's got to pay attention to his body strength. You have fifteen minutes left on your hour. Want to try that slow trot you mastered a while ago, or give your hip a rest for the day? You could take that time and walk Jack around the corral. He likes that and you'd be making a friend for the next time you come out."

The client cut a side glance at Eden and spoke a little louder. "I think I've got him calmed down. I'll walk him around the corral and become better acquainted."

Eden nodded in satisfaction. Trey was quite the salesman. Travis would've rolled his eyes and told the man he was doing it all wrong. She walked back into the house wondering how she'd react if that smooth talking voice wanted to talk her into another kind of experience.

She sighed and went to her laptop in the corner of the kitchen. If she needed a convincing pitch by Thursday, she'd better get started.

Fifteen minutes into it, she was interrupted by a knock on the door. Her second client stood on the doorstep, smiling. "Wanted you to know how much I enjoyed my ride and tell you I want to be put on your schedule as a repeat customer for the same time every week."

He handed her a check to cover the next month, then glanced in the direction of the corral. "Have to tell you I tried to hire him away. I own a nice little bar in town. He could sell *tap water* to the women who come in. Tourists or locals. He turned me down flat. No hard feelings?" Then her newest client turned and walked to his car.

Eden felt her chin drop and mentally re-examined the worth of her new employee. He'd turned down a job inside, with women lining up to flirt with him? And doubtless, more money. She smiled. She hadn't wanted to face yesterday and firing Travis, but it had turned out to be a very lucky day.

CHAPTER SIX

Trey rubbed his face with his hands. If that guy ever sat a horse in his life, Trey would eat raw oats. He chuckled. What had he expected? Eden had told him of her plan and how he would be needed, but so far, he felt like an attendant at a children's pony ride.

He thought back to Chap's suggestion that he and Eden go to Nevada to bid on another horse for their new business and pick up the gear stowed in his cabin. It really was a good idea. He wouldn't mind spending some time on the road with her, some up-close and personal time. He shook his head. Bad idea to get overly friendly with the boss. Especially since ex-cons couldn't be very choosy. Still, three years was a long time.

Thinking of Eden must have conjured her up, because there she was, walking toward the corral, a smile on that pretty face. She waved him toward the barn. "It'll be cooler in the shade."

What will? Had she received a complaint from the two clients he'd helped this morning? Nope. If so, she wouldn't be smiling. Would she?

He stepped into the shade and nearly bumped into her, his eyes adjusting to the difference in the light. "Oh, sorry."

"That's okay. I want to go over a couple of things that have come up, since you are part of the reason for both of them."

Damn. Maybe both clients *had* complained. "Anything I need to be concerned about?"

"Not at all. Both clients you helped today were happy with their experiences. The woman who rode Duster said she would be reporting back to the board that it was well worth the price. The man who rode Jack gave me a check that covered today through the end of next month. He's stoked about learning more and wanted to make sure he got the same slot on the schedule every week."

Trey was relieved. "Good news. Sounds like you'll be getting more clients from that place."

She pulled her gaze to somewhere over his shoulder. "Um that's the second thing. A client on the board was here yesterday and she, along with Ms. Williams you helped this morning, have decided in favor of letting me make a presentation to the residents. Day after tomorrow. With you."

Trey knew she was talking to and about him, but his cowboy brain didn't make the connection. "I don't get it. Do I hold up cue cards for you? Bring Duster to display the ride? How can I be helpful?"

Eden's cheeks turned pink. "Um, remember what Dad was complaining about this morning?"

He stepped back. "What? You want me to flirt with the women there?"

"No. Of course not. I'm asking you to be involved in the presentation. I intend to give a short talk then ask for questions from the attendees. We can take turns answering them."

Trey was suspicious. "And you also want me to mingle and chat them up."

Eden shrugged. "It's a sales pitch pure and simple. You made a good impression on Ms. Williams and she told the board. If it makes you uncomfortable, I'll call and tell them you can't make it."

He shook his head. What she was asking did make him uncomfortable, but she and Chap had taken a chance on him and so far, were treating him well. "I'll go, but not dressed up, and if the Williams woman corners me, you have to save me. She must do the backstroke in a tub of perfume. Made my eyes water. I tried not to, but I had to keep leaning back from her."

Eden nodded enthusiastically. "I owe you one and I promise to save you from the over-perfumed Ms. Williams." She winked. "This is the price you pay for being a 'real cowboy.'"

His mind wandered at the thought of what he would like that 'owe you one' to consist of. Eden Burris was a puzzle. A pretty woman who ran a business, seemed a fair boss, took care of her father, obviously knew horses, had a dream to own an arena, yet no boyfriend. Not enough time, nobody caught her eye, had her heart broken, been involved or married and it turned out badly, what?

Trey refocused. "Speaking of prices. Weren't you going to introduce me to your neighbor, Jenks somebody, who needs his head mare exercised?"

She put her hand on his forearm. "Yikes. I've been so worried about putting together the presentation for Desert Peace, I forgot all about Moneypenny."

Trey raised an eyebrow. "A horse named after a character in Bond movies?"

Eden tilted her head. "Wouldn't have pegged you for a movie fan."

He might be making a mistake reminding her of his recent status, but Trey shrugged. "My recent residence was essentially a macho-male population. The cooking and home decoration channels didn't get much play."

She pressed her lips together, but he saw she couldn't hold back the smile. "Makes sense. Give me a few minutes to save my presentation and log off, then give Jenks a call. I'll meet you at the end of the driveway."

Trey itched to get back on a horse and work on his roping. He knew he'd be sore with the activity, but didn't care. He loved the chase. The gamble that he and his teammate could find that perfect point and come together to shave a tenth of a second off their best time. He wondered if Eden had a partner she worked with consistently. Maybe he could talk her into working out with him, help him get back into shape. He'd have to earn a new rating, his old one had expired by now.

He used to fall into the top twenty headers on a regular basis and knew he'd have to work his way into the prize money ranks again. And before any of the top heelers would want to take a chance on him. It would also take a while to save enough for a good roping horse, and truck.

"Ready?"

Trey turned and smiled. He'd smiled more in the last couple of days than he had since the days he'd gone to greet Duster during her training. He supposed it was due to the same thing. Looking forward to seeing someone. "Ready."

He followed Eden past the next door neighbor's front door, around the house to a corral about the same size as hers. A man with a black sling on his right arm was stroking the nose of a beautiful bay with a white blaze on that nose.

Eden leaned against the corral rail. "Hey, Jenks. This is Trey Killian. Our new hand. He's looking to get some header practice in. I told him Moneypenny could use the exercise if you don't mind."

The neighbor turned and stuck out his left hand awkwardly. "Nice to meet you, Trey. Killian, you said. Why does that name ring a bell? You a roper?"

He groaned inwardly. This older man might remember, or even have been at the event where Jace had given the drugs to the horse that died. He hoped not. "Yes. Header, but I've been out of circulation for a few years."

Jenks nodded, accepting the explanation. "So, you wouldn't mind exercising this girl for me. Keeping her fit for a month or so till I get back in shape?"

Trey stepped forward and ran his hand up the bay's jaw to tickle her ear. She tossed her head and whickered. "Um, all my tack is in Nevada."

The older man sized him up. "You're about my height. You're welcome to use mine, long as you take care of it."

He thanked his lucky stars to have fallen into this area and met these people. "Great. And as long as I'll be riding on my own time; if you think of anything that needs doing while I'm here, let me know."

Jenks's gaze found Eden and he smiled. "Sight better'n that useless other one you had at your place."

Trey's new boss shrugged. "Everyone's allowed a mistake, or two. All better, now."

What was that about? Did she think he was a mistake, too? He focused on Jenks. "See you around six today?"

The man nodded and stuck out his left hand again. "Nice to meet you.'

"Same here."

CHAPTER SEVEN

Eden cut a glance at Trey on their way back to her place. The short walk enabled her to come to the conclusion Jenks was right. In a day and a half, she'd come to trust her decision to hire this ex-con, whose mistake, time-served, and subsequent appearance at her home didn't worry her. "D'you think you could spare a few minutes to go over some questions we might be asked at Desert Peace tomorrow?"

She laughed at the look on his face. He was one of those people who lived to be outdoors. It must have been overwhelming punishment to be shut in for three years. "You okay?"

Trey nodded. "Just not a fan of crowds."

Eden felt the same way most days, but his aversion to crowds meant a special kind of hell. "It's a short presentation and will answer the bulk of their questions. I don't think we'll be there long." Then her warped sense of humor won out. "Who knows, if we're successful, we might be invited to other retirement homes to give our pitch. Wickenburg is a mecca for retirees."

Oh, the desperation at the fresh horror in his look. She started to giggle. What was wrong with her?

"Haven't heard that sound in a while," Chap said, meeting them in the driveway.

Eden sobered at her dad's comment. Time for a change. She leaned down and kissed his cheek. "More where that came from, Dad. Trey's an easy target."

Trey made a face, his eyebrows drawing together. "She's picking on me. Threatening me with multiple retirement home visits and over-perfumed women."

Chap joined in her laughter. He rarely came outside when Travis put in an appearance, so, this interaction was good for him. "What's for lunch, Dad?"

"Tuna salad sandwiches and cream of tomato soup." He backed up and spun around. "One of my best dishes."

"Yeah, you've seen most of his repertoire," Eden said. "Chicken casserole, big breakfast, and now, soup and sandwich."

Trey shook his head. "Hey, I'm easy."

Eden sucked in a breath as an answer that would be embarrassing to both of them popped into her head. Her face and necked warmed. She had to stop imagining and building on innocent comments he made. And yet, she kept signing them up to spend more time together. The comment about visiting additional retirement homes could be true.

She stayed quiet through most of lunch, then put down the crust of her sandwich. "Now that you've worked with a couple of clients, what do you think of the job?"

He grinned. "Truthfully? A little boring. Not quite the same energy as roping or working a ranch. I'm grateful for the chance, though. I'll give it my best."

Eden nodded. Refreshing honesty. "If we keep the clients down to two or three a day and spend the rest of our time maintaining and improving the outfit, we could both get in more roping practice."

There it was. That devastating smile her carrot and stick, or stick and carrot had produced. Dangle the boring, then give the prize. She would have to remember his weakness to keep him around permanently. Okay, *that* was a new word when thinking about a hired hand. Rodeo and roping brought cowboys in and out of town. Trey was only the third guy she'd hired to help out since Chap's accident and he hadn't once mentioned permanence.

"I was told there's an arena not too far from here. Are the rates reasonable?"

She shrugged. "Not too bad. Thirty apiece. Gotta keep those steers fed and healthy. You can usually get in enough runs to make you tired in an hour, hour and a half."

Those magic words made his gray eyes shine. "Wanna be my heeler?"

In the worst way, she thought. In the worst way. "Sure. Middle of the week's usually not too busy."

Heaven help her when she saw him in action. Hopefully he'd be terrible and she could bow out of any further team roping arrangements. She looked again. No. He wouldn't be terrible. He'd be that little bit of wild at the jump. That, eager-to-throw the perfect rope to make the perfect catch, sex on a horse.

****

Trey felt like he'd scored. Sort of. They had a roping date. Okay, not a real date, a team practice. He hadn't even asked her if she had a regular header partner for roping practice and events. "Well, first we have to get on those questions for your presentation. We have to be sharp for that." Okay, that sounded patronizing and he hadn't really meant it to. "Actually, I have a lot to learn about the business end. I should feed Jack and Duster and then clean the barn while you put together some questions and answers to prep me. Does that work?"

He hoped so. Otherwise, there was a good chance he would make further inane statements.

Eden's eyebrows lifted. "Um, yeah. That works. See you in an hour."

Trey treated both horses to another rub down and apple slices before cleaning out the muck and adding more hay and oats to their feed boxes. He was in his comfort zone and blew out a big sigh as he stroked Duster's nose. "What's the secret, girl? How do I not mess this up?"

Duster bobbed her head and pushed at his shoulder. "Right. I'm on my own."

He went to his room, cleaned up and walked through the back door.

Eden looked up from her laptop and smiled. "Did I tell you how much I appreciate a person who's on time?"

It was just a small thing. Why did her words mean so much? "Blame my mom. She used to give me grief if I made her, or anyone, wait."

"She sounds like a good mom."

His mind took a quick detour. Yes, she had been and he missed her. "She was."

Eden's eyes cast down. "I lost my mother seven years ago. Miss her every day."

Trey hated making her sad. "What have you got for me?"

Her glance moved back to her laptop. "I put together a handout, so there won't be much information they'll need outside of that. We can build on what I have if anything comes up."

He liked it that she said we. Three days ago, he was in prison surrounded by angry, noisy men. Today, he stood in a clean, quiet kitchen speaking to a pretty woman he was hoping would find the things they had in common meant more time together. Trey pulled his mouth to one side. Shame on him. That was a big part of the reason he'd agreed to go with her to Desert Peace.

"Have a seat," Eden said, handing him a sheet of paper. "Pretend you're seventy and this is all new to you."

He hunched down and squinted at the words.

Eden laughed. "Now I know what you're going to look like at seventy. Better not let Chap see you making fun of seniors."

Trey straightened. She was right. There was one old guy in his cellblock who went by Pinochle. Always trying to scrape up a game. He was smart and really quick. No one could beat him and he was one of the few inmates Trey sought out. "Actually, I like seniors. Most of them can teach you a thing or two." Okay. That sounded condescending. "I mean . . ."

She let him off the hook, nodding at the sheet he held. "See anything on this list that needs fixing or adding?"

He gave it a quick onceover. "No. Looks good. Wait. Maybe add wear comfortable, loose clothes. Both the folks who showed today got to looking uncomfortable partway through their rides. A little overdressed."

Her eyes sparkled. "Punctual *and* observant. I'm a lucky girl."

And he was a lucky guy, Trey thought.

CHAPTER EIGHT

Eden turned to the left, then the right in front of her full-length mirror. Her gray, pencil skirt and pale coral silk shirt looked nice. She wanted to arrive business-like but not fussy. Black kid leather heels finished her outfit. Smoothing the skirt, Eden had an underlying motive in appearing nice. Trey Killian. A man who triggered her imagination and made warm swirls in her belly like no man had since her unfortunate, make that stupid, relationship of almost a year ago.

She sighed and walked toward her bedroom door. Fool me once, shame on you. Fool me twice, shame on me.

Trey would have to drive. These heels wouldn't do well operating the clutch on her twelve-year-old temperamental truck.

Chap waited by the back door. "Good luck, Honey. Knock'em dead."

Not something you want to wish on a roomful of seniors, but he knew it and meant to cheer her up. Eden smiled and picked up the folder of paperwork. "Thanks, Dad." She kissed the side of his head before leaving.

Lord help her but he was gorgeous. Trey waited by the truck. His slightly faded, dark green shirt highlighted his gray eyes. He wore freshly washed jeans and his well-worn boots shined. It looked like he'd even brushed his Stetson. She tossed him the keys. "You better take the wheel. These shoes won't do well."

He gazed down her length to her feet, and back up, grinning. She hadn't meant for him to give her the once-over, but it worked and made her smile at his pleasure. "Got it," he said.

****

They arrived at Desert Peace five minutes early and were immediately greeted by Cynthia Worden, Ms. Williams, and a younger version of her.

Thought you were safe, didn't you? Didn't count on younger women being here. This particular one wouldn't interest him, though. Eden was sure. Too pale—she didn't go outside, that would be a minus in

Trey's book. Besides, she wore too much makeup and swam in the same perfume moat as her mother. Eden straightened her shoulders. He'd figure it out. She smiled and shook hands all around.

In the next five minutes, two more age-appropriate women, another daughter, and a niece, were brought over and introduced. Trey had been polite, and charming, and all business.

Eden took the podium in Desert Peace's event room happy and relaxed. Her presentation went well. She took a chance and called on three of the people who had already ridden in the program. They all liked being the center of attention and gave glowing recommendations. At the end, she only had two questions not answered in the hand-out or through her talk. *"If I buy a horse to ride, can I stable it at your place?"* And, *"Can we take lessons as couples?"* Easy peasy.

She thanked everyone for attending and accepted multiple cheerful congratulations while keeping her mantle of business woman until they reached the parking lot. Then, Eden stopped and twirled. "We're a success!" Trey had smiled, but stayed quiet. Dying for a congratulatory hug, Eden couldn't help herself and gave Trey a quick squeeze. He gave her a quick squeeze back.

The drive back home seemed to take too long. Eden ran her hand down the sheet of paper on the clipboard she held. "Did you see? Did you see how many people signed up for time slots or were interested in taking lessons?"

Trey nodded. "I saw. We're going to be busy."

Eden felt her face warm. Her truck's cab seemed small. Had she just hugged a man she'd known for less than two days? Not just unprofessional for a boss and business owner, but a sure way to drive away your newest and most productive employee. "Um, sorry about the hands-on back there. Been working toward that break for a while and got a little too excited."

He didn't look at her. Just shrugged. "You worked hard for your success and I was handy. It's fine."

Since he seemed to be okay with her apology, Eden took advantage and offered a suggestion. "Today's response has made it pretty clear I need to leave for Nevada in two weeks. I can block out say, three days for us if you're still interested in helping out at the auction and picking up your trailer and gear. We'd only have to tow a trailer back since yours would be empty and used for the horse I intend to buy."

Trey glanced her way at the light. It was a great plan and benefitted both of them. "Sounds good. We can bunk at the cabin both nights, but who'll take over the lessons?"

Eden tapped the clipboard. "I only scheduled the next thirteen days. We'll block out three days after that if you're willing."

He pulled into her driveway and turned off the ignition. "Makes sense. I'll plan on it."

CHAPTER NINE

What Trey hadn't planned on was that hug. Nearly his undoing. He didn't think she considered a guy who'd been in prison for three dry years and the affect a hug from a pretty woman would cause. His navigation skills were good, but he made a couple of 'wrong' turns on purpose so it would take longer to get back to the Burris place while easing his discomfort.

It would be a tempting trip. Three days, with two of them long days driving down and back and one day to attend the auction and go to his cabin to retrieve his things. Actually, they would drive right to his place. They could stay in the cabin the first and second nights, dropping down to Carson City in between.

His cabin would save them from having to rent two motel rooms, but he would have to exercise great restraint. It was one big room with a bathroom enclosed in the back and a dated kitchen along one wall. Driving two long days alone with her and spending two nights alone with her had him imagining long blonde hair spread on a pillow next to him.

It was going to be a long round trip.

Arriving at the ranch, Trey turned off the ignition. "I want to check in on Moneypenny, if you don't mind. Maybe take her out. I've seen people riding on your road. If I'm back in an hour, is that okay for dinner?"

Eden nodded at him absently. "Sure. I'll let Chap know, and tell him the good news about our trip."

Trey frowned at her offhand response. He didn't think Chap would appreciate his daughter sleeping with employee in a small cabin, alone, for two nights. He shrugged. Then again, from what he'd seen, the Burrises probably had a relationship of trust. Now, all he needed was to trust *himself* around his beautiful boss.

He knocked on Jenks's door. The older man opened it, smiled and waved him around back to the barn. Moneypenny greeted him, eager for more sugar. Trey obliged. "Hey girl. Wanna go for a ride?" The horse saw him reach for the tack Jenks brought out, and danced back and forth.

Jenks laughed. "She's really been missin' gettin' out. I owe you."

Trey nodded, saddling the horse. "Not how I feel, but can I ask you a question, in confidence?"

Eyebrows up, Jenks tipped his head.

Trey stayed busy putting on the bridle. "Do you know if Eden has a boyfriend or fiancé? I haven't seen any evidence of one."

The older man looked over Trey's shoulder at his neighbor's spread. "Hard to know if I should say or not. She's good people, but maybe a little gun shy." He shrugged. "'Bout a year ago, guy she hired played up his interest in her. Real good lookin', too. Eden had been workin' so hard at the ranch and takin' care of Chap, she bought the whole package. After about three months he walked. Took a chunk of her savings with him."

Trey sucked in air through his teeth. What a jerk. "Thanks for being honest with me."

Jenks stroked his horse's neck. "Maybe I shouldn't've told you, but I'm a good judge of people and I think you're okay. Still, I'm not too old or stove up to take you on if you hurt her again."

Trey didn't laugh. "No, sir. That won't happen." He shook hands awkwardly, again, and mounted the horse. He closed his eyes with a happy sigh. Aside from the time he spent breaking and training Duster, this was the first time he'd ridden for pleasure in three years. He missed it sorely.

He gave Moneypenny her head and she walked right out onto the road. The traffic was light and the heat had built up over the day, but if the mare was willing, so was he. Friendly homeowners and ranchers waved as he passed, some even calling out the horse's name. This was the kind of place he could get used to. Spend the rest of his life in. He got Moneypenny up to a trot for a while, then turned for Jenks's place.

Eden Burris was never far from his mind. The beautiful blonde had rocked his senses for two days. It wasn't just that she was pretty and smart and turned a blue work shirt into sexy apparel, she saw people for themselves; for their work ethics, for the way they treated others, for how they handled failure. That's how he hoped she saw him.

Trey rubbed down Moneypenny and gave her some extra oats. He swore she smiled when he left.

He laughed out loud at the same casserole dish on the table from last night, tuna replacing chicken, Cream of Mushroom replacing Cream of Chicken, same crunchy potato chip topping. Chap's saving grace was serving homemade biscuits with honey. Trey loved every bite, asking what Chap planned for tomorrow night.

"Hot dog casserole, smartass."

Trey nearly choked. When he could talk again, he grinned. "Got a barbeque?"

Eden's eyes lit up. "Yes, please!"

"Barbeque once a week. My treat," Trey said. "You prefer ribs, burgers, steak, or chicken? I'm not offering hot dogs."

Chap accented his words with his fork, his chin jutted out. "It's a good thing I like you and am glad you're taking my place with the hungry widows. Otherwise, that would hurt my feelings."

Eden tipped her head. "Hope you have a large capacity for B. S., Trey. It means he likes you, though. Hot dogs, notwithstanding."

Trey expanded his earlier longing to be part of a neighborhood like this, to include Eden and Chap. Whoever the guy was that messed with Eden's feelings and stole her money, would eventually be caught and hopefully imprisoned. If not, and if pointed out, Trey wasn't beyond taking a swing at him. Not his place to do so, but it would certainly be gratifying.

****

Trey seemed a hundred miles away. Aside from discussing casseroles, the last thing he'd done was glance down at the clipboard before he left her truck.

She hadn't mentioned it, but two of the younger women had signed up for lessons. Was he checking to see if there was a name he wanted to see on the list? She hoped not. Hired help and clients was not a good idea. It troubled her that she wasn't admitting to herself that she also had a personal interest. Under control.

"I spoke to Chap about our trip to Nevada while you were with Jenks. We figure two to two-fifty in gas, plus two meals a day each at minimum, and the cost of the auction and horse. I went online and registered as a buyer, so we're set."

Trey leaned toward them. "I'd have to pay for all that out of my own pocket anyway, so, how much is my part for this trip?"

Eden should have been prepared with a number, but wasn't. In the back of her mind, she unfairly compared Trey to someone who would've let her pay for everything. "Um, you're going along to help drive and choose a horse. Picking up your trailer and gear will only be a short side trip. So, there's really no need . . ."

"No dice," he said. "I pay half the gas, for my own meals, and save us the cost of the motel rooms by using my cabin. I have a property manager. I'll call and let him know we're coming."

Eden might have known that's the way he would respond. All about fairness. She wasn't about to argue, so she lightened the mood. "You bucking for a raise already?"

Trey smiled. "I can manage, thanks." He looked around the small kitchen. "I smell cherries."

Chap crossed his arms. "Took you long enough. Made cherry cobbler for dessert. Ice cream on the side."

"You had me at cobbler," Trey said, grinning.

Eden loved his smile. There was a time when the smile of another man would have made her heart happy. Now, she had to school herself to be careful. She nodded at her father. "You get the cobbler and I'll get the ice cream,"

"Trey stood. "I can clear the table."

Eden felt her jaw slacken. *You had me at clear the table.* What the hell had Trey done to spend three years in prison?

"New set of clients starting day after tomorrow," she said. "That means cleaning day around here tomorrow. Chap does house and laundry. You do the barn and corral and your room. I split my time between the house and barn. Except for your room. Getting an early start before it gets too hot is usually best." She watched for a sour reaction, but Trey just nodded.

"Later, if you want, we can go to the arena and get in some team roping practice."

That had the effect she wanted. That, "Oh, boy, I can hardly wait," look. Very cool if those pretty gray eyes gazed at her like that.

****

Her cleaning threat took root with both Chap and Trey. Immediately after breakfast, Chap started wiping down the appliances and Trey took paper towels and glass cleaner to attack the one window in his room. Life was good.

The spare room's window faced the parcel she would love to have but couldn't afford. As she chopped and sprayed the weeds at the base of the barn, Eden came up behind him. "You may have to go at that a couple of cleaning days to get the layers off." She looked behind her. "But it'll be worth it."

Trey wore a new white t-shirt, jeans, a baseball cap and bare feet. Although she really enjoyed the view, Eden thought she should warn him. "Lots of scorpions out here, and the possibility of snakes. We spray, but can't keep them totally under control. Very painful if they get you."

He glanced down, a shade or two paler. "Been on the lookout for snakes, not the scorpions. May need to add a cheap pair of barn boots to my list of purchases. Thanks." He finished his window in a hurry and carefully stepped back to the barn.

Eden followed Trey to the door of his room. When he came out, she handed him a sheet of paper. "This is the new schedule for the next twelve days starting tomorrow. Both of us, and Jack and Duster are going to be very busy. Take a look and let me know if you have any questions."

He scanned the paper. "Thanks for taking the mother/daughter perfume duo. Needs a stronger stomach than I can manage. That and the constant chatter." Trey stopped. "Makes me sound petty and a whiner. Guess as long as I'm getting paid, I shouldn't complain so much. Sorry."

She shifted a shoulder. "I asked. Besides, I consider both those issues annoying too. As long as you don't voice them out loud to the clients, we're good. That, and if you read farther down, we're taking *turns* with the most, um, irritating of the bunch."

He threw back his head and laughed. "Fair's fair."

What wasn't fair was that his laughter and happiness elevated her own. Something she'd been trying to do on her own with small success for over half a year. And she loved it. If a man who just got out of prison could laugh at himself and his circumstances, he was quite a guy.

Later, in the arena that afternoon, he also proved himself more than capable at their sport of choice. He and Moneypenny shot out at the buzzer and moved as one to rope each steer as if they had to have one on the grill, today.

Trey complained of being rusty, but she swore there was steel under the rust and did her best to keep up. Judging from the faces of some of the other heelers and headers, they turned in some very credible times.

CHAPTER TEN

The closer it got to their trip to Nevada, the more nervous Trey got. The thing was, Eden seemed to be having the same misgivings. It was a week away, now, and yesterday, she had started to tell him something about the trip arrangements, then changed her mind. He nearly backed out twice, and thought about quitting, once.

Tonight, he couldn't sleep and decided to do laundry. Chap's and Eden's bedrooms were at the back of the little house, so, washer and dryer noises didn't bother them.

Trey washed a load and while it ran, he went back to bed and fell asleep. He woke up and went to transfer the load when Eden walked in. "Oh. I couldn't sleep and thought someone had left the light on in here." She looked half asleep, so Trey didn't think she realized she wore only a t-shirt and underpants. At first. When she did, her eyes popped open and she backed out of the room tugging at her shirt hem. Too late. Damn. Really pretty legs. Pretty toes polished in lime green, and soft blonde hair bouncing on her shoulders. *And no boyfriend. Give me strength. No. Give me that woman.*

To hell with it. He followed her into the semi-dark kitchen. The only light coming from the room they'd left. "Hey."

She turned and tugged some more. "Um, sorry."

Trey pulled out a kitchen chair and swung it between them. False security, but it worked. She stopped tugging. "What is it?"

He rubbed the top rung of the chair. Unsure if what he was about to say would be well received, upset her, or get him fired. "If we were the bar-hopping, hooking-up types, we would've slept together already. But we're not."

Eden sighed. "No, we aren't. Not that it hasn't been on my mind. A lot."

Trey smiled. Relieved that he'd been right about her feelings. "Me too. Didn't act on it because, well, I like it here and I didn't want to spoil things. Didn't want Chap, or you, to think less of me."

"I haven't helped, either," Eden said. "Telling myself over and over, by the way, that bosses and employees make bad combinations. Then scheduling you for only one lesson with Sabrina."

Trey frowned. "Who?"

"The pretty redhead. She was one of your clients, yesterday."

He'd only had three. "You mean that sort of skinny girl with all the red hair, who constantly smacked her gum? You thought she was pretty?"

Eden chuckled into the half-light. Her blonde hair a beacon. "Yes, her. Why?"

"I didn't like her. She made Duster nervous. Jerking on the reins and squealing that giggle. I'm glad I only had her for one session."

She smiled a ghost smile by the light of the range. "Oh. Well, any ideas about what we're going to do with this . . . attraction?"

Trey wanted to scoop her up and take her to his room. He sighed. "Can we start with a hug? See where that leads?" He knew where he wanted it to lead, but she'd been taken advantage of and he didn't want to push her into another regret.

Her answer was to step around the chair, slip her arms around his waist, and pull him to her.

All the want, and years without, surged through him. The physical drag her body caused nearly overwhelmed him. Then she snuggled in and it nearly killed him. He kissed her temple. "Nice."

"More than nice. Making my insides all warm and puddingie."

"Is that a word?"

"Don't care. It's how I feel." She turned her head and tilted her face to his.

It was an offer Trey wasn't about to turn down. Her body molded to his and he kissed her with all the pent-up desire he'd held back since he'd arrived. She gave as good as she got, both of them sighing and breathing heavy afterward.

"Worse than I figured," Eden said.

His happy thoughts ebbed. "Oh."

She kissed his neck. "Thought I would enjoy it, but I *really* enjoyed it. Darn."

Trey was delighted to hear she felt the same as he did. "Nope. I had no such reservations. Not one."

Eden huffed a breath. "Then, that's it."

He had trouble following her. "What is *it*?"

She gave him a quick hug and stepped back. "We're compatible. We get along, we think the same," she waved her hand between them. "And now this, this six second . . ."

She didn't have to finish. Header and heeler in perfect sync to the finish. He couldn't see her eyes, but knew there had to be a flicker of doubt, no matter how she saw the compatibility.

It was one of the hardest things he ever had to say. "I can wait. If it's really short."

Eden smiled into the grayed light and held a hand to his chest. "More than I should expect, but I need a little more time." Her hand trailed down his arm, held his hand for a squeeze, "thank you," then she went back to her room.

****

Trey turned toward the laundry room, walked a little stiffly to the washer, and transferred the clothes to the dryer. Well, that had sucked. Their relationship had certainly changed. Maybe not a hundred eighty degrees, but he understood it was going forward. He couldn't be happier for that. However, her finding out what he'd been in prison for, could ruin everything. They both loved horses and she wouldn't understand. He determined to find a good time to tell her all about it when they came home from Nevada.

He rolled over at first light and threw his arm across his eyes. Eden's schedule showed three sessions each for the next five days. Heaven help him. Trey grunted. It hadn't been all that bad. Most of the clients listened and tried to practice what he told them. A few who had been most successful in their working lives, though, thought that success extended to anything they tried. Those few were short-sighted and a little short-tempered. Used to giving instructions, not taking them. Good thing he'd recently come from a place where there was lots of one upmanship.

Eden was quiet at breakfast. Even Chap noticed it. "What is it, girl? Something bothering you? Don't start worrying 'bout your trip already. There'll be lots of good horses to choose from."

She shook her head. "It's not that. I was just thinking about that client with the new hip. He's such a know-it-all he gives me a headache. He's second on my list today."

His boss did seem unusually distracted. "I'll take him," Trey offered.

"Sorry. You're the wrong gender. Mr. 'hippy dippy' expressly requested me."

Chap put down his fork. "Grumpy or off-puttin' folks never bothered you before. Sure there isn't something else?"

"I took a call, earlier," Eden said. "Lizzie Holden."

Chap frowned. "She wanting you to give Travis his job back?"

Eden sighed and made designs in her egg yoke. "More like begged me. Apparently, he's out every night and when he's up, he whines about the way he was treated here, but thinks he'll be called back. Poor woman's ready to commit filicide."

"What's filicide?" Chap asked.

Trey toned down his grin. "Bet I can guess. Has to mean bumping off your own kid."

Eden rolled her eyes. "Right. I didn't know either, but she said she looked it up in case she has to go to jail for it."

Chap burst out laughing.

He made a heroic effort at holding it in, then Trey lost it.

Eden tried to censure them by frowning, but Trey saw her effort slipping and poked her in the ribs. "Come on. You know you want him back."

This brought renewed hysterics from Chap. "Over my dead body."

"Mine too," said Eden. "I felt sorry for her, but not sorry enough to hire Travis back."

The laughing subsided and Trey reached to tap the schedule on the table. "You don't have near enough time to yourself. Maybe when we get back from Nevada, you can hire that high school kid you've been talking about. School's almost out and you can take one on part time. Ease your load a little."

Chap nodded. "Part time's a good idea. There probably ain't a kid in this town who don't know all about horses. Besides, like Trey says, between chores, and scheduling and bookkeeping and taking care of me, you ain't got ten minutes left in the day for yourself. Let alone ropin', like you want."

She arched an eyebrow. "Well, I'm taking that ten minutes to myself this afternoon and shopping for girl stuff. No men allowed."

The thought hit Trey hard. Maybe this, sitting in a sunny kitchen with people he really liked, was the reward fate had given him for enduring the loneliness and bitter times. For acting on his belief Jace would change his ways and do right by himself. His own spur-of-the-moment decision to take the blame for dosing the horse was based on a promise to their mother he'd look out for his half-brother. Stupid and wrong way to do it. He just hoped that one mistake didn't ruin everything.

He huffed. Since when did he believe in fate? A man made his own history.

"Trey?"

His daydreaming made him miss the last thing Eden said. "Sorry. What?"

"I said, hippy dippy doesn't want to change helpers, but you could do me the favor of taking on two clients in a row. Your last, then mine. Pretty please." She added a trembling lip.

Laughter bubbled out of him again. "Can't turn down that. Sure." He reached for the schedule. "Who is it?"

Eden slid the schedule away from him with one finger. "No one important. Well, maybe a little important."

He pinched his nose. "Ms. Williams."

Eden pushed the schedule at him. "Not so bad as that . . . Chap, get back here."

Surprisingly, the older Burris's chair had a high gear, and Chap had it revved up. He slowed to turn and face her. "It's Cynthia Worden, isn't it? And you want me to soften her up first, because she likes to be treated special by 'the owners.' "

"Good by me," Trey said, meaning it. He had no time or patience for people like Cynthia.

CHAPTER ELEVEN

They were leaving first thing in the morning. Eden mapped out a drive with breaks for eating and gas. Each taking four-hour turns. Otherwise, it was straight through to Carson City and then Incline Village to his cabin. She had looked up the area online and was amazed to see million and multi-million-dollar houses on the north end of Lake Tahoe. It made her nervous. What if Trey's "cabin" was really an expensive home? Eden shook her head. No. What would he be doing here, mucking out stalls, working with seniors and eating the same boring food Chap served day after day?

His cabin was the big question. Staying there for two nights alone with Trey would be a challenge she hoped she was up to. Almost a week ago she had asked him to wait, but hadn't said how long. She didn't consider herself a tease, but he didn't know how bad she was hurt a year ago by a charming, good-looking cowboy who'd seen her vulnerability and taken advantage. She knew in her heart Trey wasn't that kind of man, and she would trust her heart that this time she was right.

Unfortunately, all these thoughts looping through her head were keeping her from getting the sleep she needed for the long trip ahead.

Eden covered her yawn the next morning, twice, while they were loading the truck. She noticed Trey yawning too. "We're a pair to be on the road. Both half asleep."

He huffed a breath. "Sorry. Lots of details going through my brain. Didn't sleep well."

She pulled her mouth to one side. "Me either, but we'll be fine."

****

Eden drank too much coffee before they left and had to take a bathroom break before they made their first stop and driver switch. Boy, was she tired, and the excess caffeine didn't allow her to nap. When her turn to drive came, she had to stay wide awake and took the opportunity to study Trey, who had no such problem falling asleep and snored lightly. By the time her shift was over, and Trey took the last couple of hours, Eden conked out in the corner of her seat.

She woke up at Trey's gentle nudge, and peered through the windshield. Her brain had conjured up a little log cabin in the woods. This was a small house surrounded by haphazard growth, not a log cabin. A shack would have been a better description. Six-hundred square feet at best, with a dim light showing through one of two windows on the front wall.

Trey peered at the window. "That's interesting. I told my property manager to keep the power on so the place had heat and the pipes wouldn't freeze. I wonder why there are lights on too."

Eden smothered a yawn and realized her thighs were numb. "Maybe you have a squatter. Still patchy snow up here. Summer must be a real short season."

Trey's gaze moved to the left of the structure where the back end of what looked to Eden like a brand-new pickup stood. "A squatter with money?" he asked.

They got out of the truck, and Trey held up a hand. "Give me a sec, okay?"

Eden stomped her feet and tried to rub feeling back into her legs. "Sure. But be careful."

Trey walked to the window and peered in, stopping to shake his head before turning. He went back to Eden's truck. "Good news, bad news. Good news is, it's my brother Jace. That's also the bad news."

Interesting that Trey thought the appearance of his brother could be bad news. She'd wait for the explanation. "So, you co-own the cabin?"

Trey shook his head again, but Eden couldn't see the expression on his face in the dark. He pulled his duffle from behind the driver's seat. "Nope. It's all mine. Left to me by my grandfather on my dad's side. Guess I'll find out what Jace is doing here. And how he got in."

Eden was wide-awake at this revelation. Trey also thought his brother, okay half-brother, broke into his cabin? She scrambled to grab her overnight bag and follow him to the door.

He turned the knob and the door opened easily. Unlocked. Eden looked into a room in disarray. As she trailed him in, she also noticed it smelled like Travis's room. Dirty clothes and dirty dishes. A younger, slim, but not as good-looking version of Trey lay sprawled on the single bed.

Trey suspended his duffle over Jace's midsection, then released it. It landed with a whump.

Eden winced as the younger man folded upward. ". . . wha?"

Jace knocked the duffle away and swung his legs over the side of the bed, scrubbing his face with his hands. When his eyes cleared, he jumped up and grabbed Trey in a hug. "Bro! Where've you been? I showed up for your release and missed the day by one."

"Typical. I got a job in Arizona," Trey said, then stepped back. "What are you doing in my cabin?"

Jace grinned. "Ran into some bad luck about a week ago. Decided this would be a cozy place where no one would find me."

"How did you get in?"

"Oh. You gave me that property manager's name for emergencies. I called him and he came out with a key."

Eden decided she didn't much care for Trey's brother. Her instinct was borne out when he looked around Trey and saw her. "For me? You shouldn't have."

Trey gritted his teeth. "Don't be an ass. This is Eden Burris, my boss."

Jace bobbled his eyebrows at that.

Eden set her bag down and turned. "I'm going to lock up my truck."

Trey spoke softly. "What the hell, Jace? What's been going on that you have to hide? Are you in trouble again?"

Outside, Eden counted to ten, stomping her feet in the cold, then locked her truck. As she went back in the cabin, Jace was slapping Trey on the back. "So, you see, all fixed with a little cash."

"How little?"

Jace winked at Eden, ignoring Trey's question. "Did you see my new truck out there? Beauty, isn't it? Fresh off the showroom floor and only about a hundred miles on it. Like that deep blue color?" He stepped closer to her. "Kinda matches your eyes."

Eden didn't even hesitate. The self-defense classes she's taken a couple of years ago popped into her head and she drove the heel of her hand into his solar plexus. Jace dropped like a sack of potatoes. The unghhh sound he made was satisfying. She dusted her hands. "Don't like your brother much. Sorry."

Trey burst out laughing. "I don't blame you and nothing to be sorry about. I'd almost forgotten what a jackass he can be. Leave him there. I'll change the bedding if you throw a load of dishes in the sink to soak. Jace and I'll roll out sleeping bags on mats and you can have the bed once it's cleaned up. Work for you?"

Yes, it did. She was a little surprised Trey had chosen her over his brother and she felt bad about it. For about a nanosecond. She reached to peck his cheek. "Absolutely."

Trey gave her a quick hug. Eden couldn't be a hundred percent sure in the dim light, but she thought there was a twinkle, and something personal for her, in his eye. That worked too.

****

Trey rolled over in his sleeping bag. The half-light of early morning picked out Eden's blonde hair on her pillow. He thought of it, the pillow, the bed, heck, the entirety of what he owned as hers. She was amazing and his feelings for her got stronger every day. They'd walked into a mess made by Jace though, and he was tired of cleaning up after his half-brother, figuratively *and* literally. Unless Jace's life was in danger, it stopped now.

The bathroom here was even smaller than the one he had at Eden's place, but he managed to clean up decently and leave the room wiped down for her. When he walked out, Jace still slept the sleep of the unencumbered. Guile, or most likely luck, keeping him a step ahead of getting the stuffing kicked out of him, or worse. Well, that was poetic and to complete the picture.

Eden stood at the tiny stove, cooking eggs and bacon from the groceries they'd brought with them.

She turned and smiled. "I'll clean myself up after breakfast. Then I want to arrive early to look over the available horses. That okay with you?"

Trey nodded. "Fine."

Eden tipped her head toward the still snoring Jace. "Leave him be?"

CHAPTER TWELVE

Trey's guts tightened on seeing some of the prison personnel at the auction. He'd had to work for them as a prisoner, now he was here, with a beautiful woman, to bid on a horse just like any other buyer. He received nods and even a handshake from most of them, then relaxed. Until he realized several of the others were cutting glances at Eden. He didn't blame them, but threw back looks that made them aware he didn't appreciate their interest.

Eden picked out two mares, both around the same age as Duster. She leaned into Trey, speaking low. "I'm going to bid on number three, and if I lose out, I'll bid on number five."

Trey looked at the paperwork. Eden had seen something special about Duster and he agreed she had noticed the same spirit in the two horses she mentioned.

Either would make fine head horses too. He patted the cash in his pocket. If the bidding got a little steep, he was prepared to help out. But only if she really needed it. He was fast realizing Eden's independence meant a lot to her.

Turned out he didn't need to offer his help. Eden opened strong and her competition got the vibe right away she meant to have this horse. At the close of the bidding, she released a sigh. "That was close to my limit. Buyers are figuring out this auction is a good source for well-trained horses."

"Men who trained them take a lot of pride in their work," Trey said.

"They should," Eden said, smiling and stepping up to pay for the horse she'd won.

Trey waited while the paperwork was done and smiled when Eden walked back, a big grin on her face. "We can load Lolly any time by the close of the auction."

He closed his eyes. "Lolly? Can't you change her name to something more, I don't know, substantial? Like Brunhilde, or Warrior Girl?"

Eden put her hands over her ears, laughing. "Stop. I'm going to have an accident. Besides, I was told the man who trained her named her after his daughter. I'm not changing it."

Trey pulled Eden's hands away from her ears. "Fairs, fair. How about an early lunch? My treat." He smacked his chest with his fist. "I need big protein to face my brother. He's a wild man with no restraints. He made me empty promises before I went in and I need to know his real plans before I kick him out."

Eden stopped laughing. "Okay. Big protein it is. But I get to celebrate winning Lolly by having dessert."

And she did. Trey enjoyed eating something besides soup and sandwich. Especially with his very pretty boss. His idea of dessert, before facing Jace. It would be ugly, but his brother had to be cut loose and that cutting loose would come with a lecture and an ultimatum.

****

It was as if he and Eden had never cleaned. Beer bottles and dirty dishes littered the short counter by the sink and unused perishables sat on top of the tiny fridge.

He opened the fridge door and traded a carton of half and half for one of the beers. "Those groceries were inside here for a reason."

Jace grunted. "Needed room for the beer. Can't stand the taste of warm beer."

Trey huffed a breath. "I'm going to take care of Eden's new horse. When I come back, we're going to talk."

Jace snickered. "Ex-con to badly behaved brother. That should be interesting. Think I'll have another beer to fortify myself." He winked. "Maybe not. I have an appointment coming at four."

Trey didn't believe him. "You're inviting people out to my cabin now?" He flapped his hands. "Never mind. I'll deal with it when your *appointment* shows." He nodded to Eden, then turned and left.

Spending time with a well-trained horse gave him peace. He off-loaded her, walked her around the grounds, letting her smell and see things while talking softly, then rubbed her down, put a horse blanket on her and added more feed in the trailer before reloading her.

He pulled up his cell phone and checked the time. Three-thirty. He took a deep breath. Jace probably invited a woman over to spend the evening. And possibly the night. Trey figured he'd be a very unpopular host when he asked them to leave.

Inside, Eden had started clearing up.

"You don't have to do that," Trey said. "Jace needs to clean up after himself. Right, Jace?"

His brother held up a beer in toast. "Rather watch a pretty woman do it."

"I know it sounded like I was giving you a choice, but I wasn't. Eden is a guest, here. Either you do it, or your *appointment* is going to arrive and find you flat on your ass."

Jace's eyes widened and he bowed in Eden's direction. "Of course. But Trey here will need to apologize when he finds out my surprise."

Eden walked to stand by Trey. "I don't believe he will."

The measure of happiness that came to Trey astonished him. He put an arm around Eden and pulled her close. "What she said."

Jace's grin faded until they heard a knock at the door. His grin re-lit as he went to answer it, waving an arm at Eden. "I'll see your blonde and raise you a redhead." He swung the door open and there stood a beautiful redhead. One thing was wrong. This woman was way out of Jace's league.

She stepped inside and held out her hand. "Nice to see you again, Jace." Then she turned to Trey, sizing up Eden with a measure, and returning her gaze to Trey. "You must be Mr. Killian. I'm Aileen Kendrick. Hopefully, Jace has told you about my offer."

Trey couldn't imagine Jace affording anything this woman had to sell, but before he expressed his puzzlement, Jace threw his arms in a touchdown stance and yelled, "We're rich."

Aileen Kendrick settled a pleasant smile on her mouth. "Jace contacted me a few days ago concerning your property here. As you probably know, Incline Village enjoys a prosperous population with multi-million-dollar homes as a standard."

Trey figured with two witnesses to murder, he should probably not kill Jace where he stood. He nodded at the woman. "I'm afraid you're wasting your time. This property is not for sale, Ms. Kendrick."

Her glance slid to Jace. "That wasn't my understanding. I was told my offer of two million would be gladly accepted. If that's not the case, well . . .the fifteen-thousand-dollar binding advance you received will have to be returned."

Trey stayed silent. If he read the situation correctly, Jace put the money down on a new truck and blew off the people he owed gambling losses to.

Eden hadn't said anything. It was just like her to mind her own business and not interrupt.

Ms. Kendrick pulled a card from her expensive coat's pocket and handed it to Trey. "Offer's still open. Oh, and if you get a better one, let me know and I'll do my best to top it."

When Jace closed the door after her, Eden leaned toward Trey's ear. "I didn't like the way she said 'offer,' to you. A little too friendly."

He would've been overjoyed at Eden's remark, but he was still reeling at the two million dollar offer for the horse acre and cabin his grandfather had left him. At least he owed Jace for bringing that to his attention. Something to think about now that he had a relationship with Eden.

Trey turned to Jace, whose bubble had truly burst. "Start from the beginning."

Jace shrugged, showing no remorse for the lies told and expectations flattened. "Like Aileen said. I contacted her after finding a bunch of business cards and flyers from realtors had been shoved through the mail slot. I had no idea the place would be worth as much as she said, but she typed up a contract and signed it as good will." He waved his arm around the cabin. "Can't believe you aren't willing to sell this dump for two million. I was only going to ask for five percent for setting it up. You're a real drag, Trey." He shook his head. "I have a week's full down payment return option on the truck. I'll take it back today." His gaze found Eden, his mouth twisted in anger. "Not sure what your story is, but hooking up with this guy's a mistake. Did he tell you he's an ex-con?"

Trey gritted his teeth. He knew Jace was lazy, a drinker, and gambled way over his means, but wouldn't have expected this level of betrayal. "That's enough, Jace. I'm sorry you got yourself into this mess, but you shouldn't have gone ahead without finding me. How did you expect to carry it off? The property is in my name only."

"That's just it, Bro. I couldn't pass up a deal like that and couldn't find you."

Trey knew that was a lie. "Doesn't wash. You used the property manager's number to get him out here with a key, but didn't ask him how to contact me. I called to make sure."

Jace looked somewhere over Trey's shoulder. "Small mistake on my part, Bro. Won't happen again."

Trey sighed. Still a liar, still not taking responsibility. He turned to Eden. "Can we have a few minutes?"

She nodded. "Of course. I want to visit Lolly anyway."

CHAPTER THIRTEEN

Eden stood by Trey's old trailer embarrassed by the conversation she could hear clearly, as though the windows were made of tissue paper.

"We're done, Jace. I mean it. This is one too many times you've stepped in it and I'm not coming to the rescue. I have a good job and live with people I like. I'm getting back on my feet."

"Hey," Jace said, his voice tight with anger. "No harm, no foul. I didn't ask you for money. Just told you I was tapped out. I've managed to stay on my feet the three years you were inside. So, I'll pack up and get out of your way. Give you and blondie some privacy."

Eden winced. She hated seeing the brothers, however much she didn't care for Jace, split up. He was all the family Trey had, even though a visit to Alcoholics Anonymous wouldn't hurt.

Trey's voice sounded tired. "Not necessary. And as I said, her name is Eden. We're leaving early in the morning. Just make sure you're out by the end of the day. And Jace? I'm sorry things didn't work out."

Eden heard some plate or glass break against the wall. "You're kicking me out for real? She knows you're an ex-con. But does she know you were sent to prison for dosing a horse that died?"

Blood rushed to Eden's head and pounded in her ears. Trey killed a horse? On purpose? There must be a mistake. She walked to the door and opened it with a trembling hand. "You were sent to prison for killing a horse? No wonder you didn't want to *share*."

He stood staring at her. Pain in his eyes. "Please."

Eden stood stock still. How could she fall for a loser again? Only this time he didn't just take her money, he took her faith. All of it. "Yes, or no?"

"That was the charge, yes. And I pled guilty to it, but . . ."

She interrupted in a voice she didn't trust. "I'll leave the trailer here tonight and stay at a motel. I'll rent a trailer tomorrow morning and be back to pick up my horse. By the way, you're fired."

"Eden, wait."

She walked to the truck, unlatched the hitch, and drove off without answering him. The last thing she heard before slamming her truck door was Jace's laughter.

****

The racket wouldn't stop. There were multiple conventions in town and the conventioneers had made party noises for hours. Fine with her as she'd cried herself out and couldn't sleep anyway. Eden looked at the clock. They'd finally quieted down two hours ago. What was this new nonsense? It sounded like someone was banging on her door. She hoped the place was on fire, because that was the only way she would open it. "Go away."

"It's me, Jace. I been to every motel in town looking for you. I have to talk to you."

"No, you don't. Takes two people to have a conversation. I'm not one of them."

The partier in the room next to hers had the nerve to bang on the wall and shout, "Shut up. Do you know what time it is?"

If her eyes hadn't been swollen from crying, Eden would've rolled them. She turned on the light, broiling her eyes, and punched the button on the phone designated for the front desk. No answer. And the banging continued.

"Answer your damn door," her neighbor begged.

The trailer rental place didn't open until nine-thirty. She could still get five hours of sleep after killing Jace to silence him. She stalked to the door and jerked it open. "What!"

Jace leaned against the doorjamb. Alone. "He's not here. Doesn't have any idea. Spare me five minutes and I'll go away forever if you want. I promise."

Eden started to say something, but Jace continued. "For what my promise is worth, I really mean it this time, you know?"

Her brain pinched. "No, I don't, please lower your voice and tell me why you're here, in fifty words or less. Preferably, less."

Jace stood away from the doorjamb and shoved out a breath. "Trey went to prison for me."

Eden shook her head. "How is that even possible?"

He found the cuticle on his thumb interesting. "I lost big in Las Vegas playing poker with some guys I didn't know. In return for what I owed, they would either break both my legs, or, since the international rodeo was in town, I could dose a horse in the roping event, to slow her reaction time. They would bet on another team to win." He shrugged. "I'm basically a coward, so I took the syringe they gave me and administered all of it. I was only supposed to give her half, but I thought more would be better. The horse died. Trey found out and knew if I was convicted, I'd never get into veterinary school. I begged him to help me and promised to give up gambling and drinking and go back to college. He believed me and turned himself in. Unfortunately, the judge was an animal lover. Trey got the max. More than fifty words. Sorry." He cut me a quick look. "And sorry I made you sad. Trey said you're pretty terrific."

Stunned is a good word. So is conflicted. Stunned and saddened to know anyone would think of hurting a beautiful animal like a horse to win a bet. Conflicted about her feelings for Trey now that he said she was terrific. But, did he really think going to prison for Jace would change his brother's personality and make him a good guy? "What's the moral to this fairy tale?"

Jace now studied the pattern in the carpet. "That? Oh. He said he was stupid to have made the bargain in the first place and look what it had cost him and was still costing him. And we really were done for good unless I came up with a plan worth listening to."

Okay. Respect was shining through the black moment. "What have you come up with?"

"Uh, cut back on the beer and get a real job?"

"Not exactly a master stroke." I sigh. "Come in."

****

Jace met her in the motel parking lot four hours later. And gritty eyes or not, she followed him to the dealership where he turned in the new truck and got his down payment and his beat-up old truck back. Next stop real estate office. Then, back to the cabin.

Trey's face appeared at the window when Jace and Eden rolled down the overgrown gravel driveway. Jace got out and knocked on the cabin door, Eden followed. His brother answered, a puzzled frown in place. Jace went in and turned, arms folded. Trey wasn't watching him, though, he kept his gaze on Eden. She nodded at the younger brother. "Jace has something to say."

That was all she could manage as Trey reached around her to close the door. That damned white t-shirt and form-fitting jeans thing distracted her. This time with a fresh fragrance of shower thrown in. Eden took a deep breath.

Trey focused on Jace. "What's going on?"

His brother unfolded his arms and rubbed his fingers across his thumbs. "I had this idea. Tell Eden what really happened and see if that would help, you know, the situation. So, I went to about a million motels until I found her."

Trey turned his attention to her. His expression solemn. "And?"

Eden put fisted hands on her hips. "We're getting to it, but first, *what were you thinking?*"

Trey leaned to rub a gentle thumb under her eye. "I wasn't. Just shot from the hip . . . You've been crying. I'm sorry."

That was nearly her undoing, and she didn't need a reminder of how bad she looked, but Chap's daughter was made of sterner stuff. "Not important. Are you willing to listen?"

He shrugged. "Jace knows what I expect from him. I told him not to come back unless he was ready to deal with me straight up."

Jace moved from one foot to the other. "Already told her it was stupid, Bro. She thinks so too and wants to know if we're going to follow through on the plan we came up with. Because you haven't been around, my fault, for three years to keep me from being stupid, I realized I can't go back to that. If you don't like this plan I'm willing to do whatever."

Trey moved his gaze between her and Jace. "We have a plan?"

"Mostly hers," Jace admitted. "But I'm okay with it. If it squares things with you."

Eden nodded. "You know how I told you to put the horse manure in that big, galvanized tub in the corner of the last stall? A landscaper in Phoenix picks it up for a special mixture of fertilizer he composts. Anyway, he's always complaining about needing helpers. Guys he can trust to do the heavy lifting, and eventually train to go on jobs by themselves. The pay's decent and although the work's hard, it's a start. Jace is interested and willing to take pictures of his check every week and text them to you to assure you he got paid. He needs a loan to get a place to live and will pay that person back in the first six months of working. What do you think?"

Eden watched as Trey's expression turned to hopeful. He looked at Jace. "It's hard, dirty work. Sure you want to do this?"

Jace shifted a shoulder. "Got nothing else to do and no one to do it for. 'Sides, might make up a little for not coming to visit you since I was ashamed to. And less beer might knock some of the jackass out of me." He shook his head. These last three years have sucked, man."

Trey took Eden's hand. "How do we put this plan into action?"

"Guy I owe the poker money to was all about my ostrich-skin cowboy boots," Jace said. "Those'll cancel that debt, but leave me tapped out." He grinned. "And barefoot."

Eden added to the momentum. "I talked to the landscaper this morning. He needs you right away. Says you can stay in a small apartment over his garage until you find a place you can afford."

Trey grinned. "I brought five-hundred-dollars in case Eden needed help getting the horse she wanted. I can spare four-hundred for you to buy gas, food, and some work boots, until you get your first paycheck. Easy on the beer."

Eden squeezed his hand. Trey had brought money to make sure she got what she wanted. Now, he was trusting his irresponsible brother with what she figured was most of his cash, so Jace could get a fresh start. Good-looking, not lazy, loved by animals, . . .she could go on and on about the man she was falling in love with. "It's you and me and Lolly and a long day ahead."

****

A year later, and six months into married life, Eden and Trey sat on the new patio that led from the master bedroom addition. They watched the construction crew putting in the gates for the arena on their parcel next to the ranch. Trey had sold the cabin and bought the parcel for her as a wedding present. The best of his life was ahead of him and he hugged his wife every chance he got. They were also turning out to be a great roping team.

Jace had proved true to his word. He had worked hard, cut back on the booze, stopped gambling, and built Eden and Trey a beautiful garden pergola as a wedding gift. He was a frequent visitor to their home and his gambling took the form of playing cards with Chap. Even though the older man warned Jace he cheated.

"Sad today." Eden said, grinning. "Cynthia Worden's last lesson. Chap's a broken man."

"I can help you feel better," Trey said, crooking an eyebrow. "Anytime, Mrs. Killian."

The End

AUTHOR BIO

DeeAnna is a freelance editor and travel agent for happy endings (romantic suspense, women's fiction, children's picture books and mysteries). She writes and teaches for the love of it, has never met a dog she did not want to pet, or a pie she did not want to taste. She lives in eastern Washington State wine country with her husband, and a miniature pinscher ~ Pandora the naughty goddess. DeeAnna tries to live life without props.

Other Titles by this author

Published by The Wild Rose Press

Gambling on the Goddess

McCarren's Rules ~ Angel Falls

Self-Published

Beach Reads (anthology)

Christmas Reads (anthology)

Delta on my Mind

Chasing Glory

Ellori's Fine Adventure (children's book)

The Crown of Everything (children's book)

Jewel in the Garden

Darcy Carson

DEDICATION

To my friend, Judy Williams. Thank you for all the hours of listening to me rant about my characters and letting me use your family members' names.

CHAPTER ONE

Madden Westerdahl sat in his cluttered office on the family tulip farm in Skagit Valley Washington. He read and reread the letter until stars appeared before his eyes. Damn persistent salesman. The guy never quit. This had to be the fifth—sixth letter he'd received offering to purchase the property. He had no intention of opening any type of communication with—he glanced at the signature on the bottom—C.J. Brooks of Staple Construction.

How dare the guy refer to his work as a job. What Madden did was a labor of love.

In some way the tactic reminded him of a realtor who called a house a house to disassociate the owner from the residence when selling, and a home when a potential buyer showed interest. Simple semantics.

"I don't care what he has to say. I'm not talking to him. Ever," he grumbled aloud to himself, wadding the paper up and throwing it into the wastebasket alongside his desk.

Gizmo, a mixed breed of German Shepherd and English Bulldog, raised his head at the noise. The dog looked from the basket to him, then laid his head back down.

Madden had worked the fields outside the window during wet springs, hot summers and crisp falls over half his life, graduating, going off to college, even a stint in the army. Since the 1900s Westerdahls tilled the soil, putting blood, sweat, and tears into the fertile land. He wasn't any different from those early farmers. He planned to restructure and recreate the agricultural phenomenon of tulips until the world took notice.

A glance out the window revealed ten months of preparation. Even though only mid-February, spring beckoned with hundreds of green tulip tips. By April a kaleidoscope of iconic blooms in rows of bright yellow Sunshines, Ali Baba reds, Snowflake whites, Pretty Princess pinks and fringed Burgandy Laces would create a virtual rainbow over the landscape.

A knock on the door broke his concentration. "Come in."

Wagging his tail, Gizmo rose to greet foreman Todd Olszewski in his traditional flannel shirt and ball cap as he stepped inside. Bent with age, he'd been hired decades ago, and seen every disaster that could happen in a tight business, like tulips.

"There's a call on the retail line for you," he said, scratching the dog behind the ears.

"Who is it?"

"Someone from Staple Construction."

Madden's gut rolled. "You, better than anyone, shouldn't encourage me to communicate with them. They want to buy the farm and bulldoze over the flowers, build residential houses or a mall. You'd be out of a job."

"Maybe I'm ready to retire."

Madden sat straighter. "Well, I'm not ready to sell. Tell whoever it is I'm not in."

A look of pity crossed Todd's weathered face. "You're going to have to speak with them some time."

His frustration sky-rocketed. "Like hell I do."

Todd stepped forward, bringing the hint of moist earth and chilly air with him. "The tulip economy is in freefall. You can't keep dumping money you don't have into this place."

Madden knew the old man loved the farm as much as him and walked the rows every morning, many times before sunrise. "I can get creative. I'll come up with an idea."

"Look, boss. I know this place means the world to you. You came home and have tried to build it into a thriving business. That's something to be proud of. It's not your fault the economy sucks. You're gonna have to face reality sooner or later."

The financial crisis he faced wasn't something Madden wanted to discuss. "Geez, thanks. Why don't you take your cheery outlook away and leave me alone?"

Todd continued to press. "What if those yokels in Mount Vernon's Chamber of Commerce decide to close the tulip festival?"

"They haven't cancelled in over three decades."

"That doesn't mean they won't this time. Ninety percent of our revenue comes during March and April. You can't afford to take another financial hit like last year. What'cha gonna do?"

Madden hated when the old man was right. "Keep my fingers crossed."

****

Cobie Brooks hit the off button on her cell and placed it atop her desk. She inhaled deeply. He wouldn't take the call. To say frustration twisted her inside out was putting it mildly. The owner of the four-hundred acre farm in Mount Vernon wasn't making her job easy. The tulip farm was the perfect location for an active adult community of over fifty-five. A clubhouse with an indoor pool, exercise room, gathering rooms for classes, and a wine club. The homes would be placed in a way to accommodate miles of bike and walking trails. Homeowners would find everything they desired.

All the plans were set.

Well, except for one thing.

First, she had to contact the elusive farm owner and convince him into accepting her company's offer, which was more than fair in her opinion. It would be an uphill battle because a lot of emotion was involved with generational landowners. From experience, she knew logic was the best persuader.

Right!

She'd received a tip that the owner might be suffering financial difficulty, especially if the month-long tulip festival was cancelled. Never one to let a good opportunity pass, she'd tried to talk with him about selling his land. Both her and this…this Madden Westerdahl could come out ahead. In fact, they both would—her with a chance to turn the deal into the next step in her career of becoming a construction project manager and him with a fatter bank account.

Her gaze fell on a book she kept on her desk entitled Swaying People. She'd practically memorized every word within its pages. The book put her on the path to figuring out how people made money in the real estate market. She wasn't particularly fond of being in sales. Few people trusted salesmen, or in her case—saleswomen. This gave her the opportunity to fix the perception. She'd majored in marketing with a minor in advertising and combined those learned skills with the book to make the best deals and deliver results for her employer and enjoy life at the same time. The advice had never failed her…until now.

In regards to this tulip farmer, she'd written several letters attempting to form a connection, and had yet to hear from him. Sellers usually refused to deal because they considered an offer too low. Not in this case. No offer had been extended.

That's why she decided to start calling. Make it personal. Contacting an individual was a delicate balance in the world of sales. Too little interface came across as a lack of interest. Plus, people had a tendency to forget. Too much could be interpreted as bullying and people usually balked at the trait.

While good at her job—marketing and advertising—this was brand new territory for her. She'd switched to land acquisition for Staple Construction recently and while she'd made several small deals, this was her first major test. She ran her fingers through her hair, glad she kept it shoulder-length and straight.

Allowing herself a moment of calm, she stood up, grabbed her purse, and slipped into her coat.

Her co-worker, Yvonne LeClaire, looked away from her computer screen. She had been recently promoted into project management, a real achievement in the male dominated field. "Where you going?"

"Time to charge full steam ahead."

"Which means what?" Yvonne had worked alongside Cobie the last four years. They respected each other's skills, and had become close friends, sharing the same determination to succeed in the world of construction management. Few women did. In fact, Cobie had recently read of a young lady receiving a 'hard hat' upon graduating with a degree in the field from her male classmates.

Cobie shook her head. "A drive north and an in-person visit is called for to convince that stubborn owner to sell his property."

"Be careful. This morning the weatherman predicted a snowstorm."

"It's February. It won't snow."

Yvonne beamed a crooked grin. "You're one stubborn Irishwoman. I'm just warning you. You're from Arizona and we haven't had a really bad winter since you moved here. Historically, January and February are the snowy months in the Pacific Northwest."

"Then pray it holds off. My car, BB, isn't built for snow."

"Maybe you should stay here...just to be safe. Try calling again."

Cobie hoped Yvonne was wrong...for BB's sake. "Already made up my mind."

****

Madden stopped in his tracks when he spotted a drop-dead gorgeous woman browsing an aisle in the retail store at the front of the farm. For a second, his heart raced when he thought it was his ex-girlfriend. No, it wasn't Carolyn. She'd been high maintenance from their first date and their relationship hadn't ended well. Once he got over the shock, he blinked to clear his vision.

Who was she? Few people visited this early in the season.

His heart rate returned to normal, and he took a moment to enjoy the sight of the long-limb blonde stroll around the store, and read labels on last year's crop of bulbs. She took particular notice of the new colors his father had developed—an almost lime green he named

Judy's Pistachio Dessert after his mother and a creamy white with double rows of frilly petals called Aunt Wanda for her naturally curly hair. Naming flowers after family members was a tradition started by his grandfather.

Moving away from the bins, she passed the stand with free coffee for customers, fingered a multi-spotted vase that was the perfect size for cut flowers and would work with various colors.

She was dressed more formally than the usual tourists who visited in jeans or sweats when the fields were in full bloom. This woman wore a daffodil yellow woolen pant suit with black trim that tapered to a narrow waist that shouted business woman in his mind. Her hair was one of those fringe dos cut in a bob style with bangs—not long, not short. He liked how it framed her heart-shaped face.

Shaking his head, he snapped out of his reflection and walked to the counter where Susan, a retired librarian, manned the cash register. Gizmo opened his eyes but didn't bother to lift his head from where he'd settled on his bed under the counter.

"Susan, there's a customer at the other end of the store who might need assistance making a decision about her purchases. Would you mind checking on her? I'll man the register."

CHAPTER TWO

Cobie smiled at the approach of an older woman. The badge hanging from a lanyard and cream apron with a soil spot above the pocket identified her as an employee.

"Hi, there. Can I help you find anything on this fine Friday?" the woman asked in a pleasant tone.

Cobie put down the spotted vase she'd been admiring. "This is such an interesting store. I've never visited here before. Think I made a mistake."

"You found us now. We're the Northwest's premier tulip farm in the valley. We have the largest selection of bulbs in the entire state. Plus, we sell multiple varieties of daffodils and crocus as well. Can I help you find anything particular?"

"I certainly hope so. I'm looking for the owner of the store. Can you direct me to him?"

A huge smile flashed on the woman's face. "I can do you better than that. Follow me. I'll take you right to him." When Cobie hesitated to pick up the vase again, the woman waited, then said, "Bring it along if you want. I'll hold it at the register for you."

The helpful employee made meeting the owner easier than Cobie predicted. She'd expected resistance. "Thank you. This is very kind of you."

"All my pleasure."

The woman led her to the register located at the front of the store. A tall man with shaggy blond hair, storm grey eyes, and ruggedly handsome features stood behind the counter. He hadn't been there when she entered. She would have noticed.

"This lady wants to meet you, Madden," said the older woman, fading back, deliberately leaving Cobie alone with him.

Several expressions passed over his face— bewilderment, suspicion, amusement before settling on a neutral look. Then he flashed a genuine smile and his already handsome face transformed into something beyond description.

"Hello. What can I do for you? Er... Miss..."

"Oh, sorry. I'm Cobie Brooks. Thank you for seeing me." She set the vase on the corner of the counter, shifting into full-on business mode.

Rows formed on his forehead as if confused. "Madden Westerdahl. What's this all about? Do we know each other?"

"Not yet, but I hope we can become better acquainted. Let's start with you calling me Cobie."

His frown lessened the tiniest bit. "Only if you call me Madden."

"Nice name," she replied without thinking, then thought, unique too. Probably a family name. .

"Thanks. It's a family name."

So, she'd guessed right. Maybe it was an omen for a good start, even if it sounded like she was hitting on him, which would have been fine if this meeting wasn't about business. Driving I-5 from Kirkland through rolling hills to Mount Vernon took a little over an hour and had been the right decision as far as she was concerned. It gave her time to prepare numerous contingencies. This was just the start.

"It's finally nice to meet you." She stuck out her hand.

He stared at the proffered hand, then his gaze flicked to the female employee standing in front of the cash register who pretended not to eavesdrop on their discussion. He took her hand, his grasp firm. "Excuse me. I think you have me at a disadvantage. If we met before, I'm sure I would have remembered you."

Cobie gave him a firm shake. "I'm sorry. I didn't mean to give the impression that we'd met."

"Oh, that's a shame," he answered, sounding disappointed. "Maybe we should take this conversation somewhere else and you can tell me what this is all about."

"Outside. It's a bit nippy, but the sun is shining in all its glory." She glanced at the female employee. "Can you hold this vase for me? I'll be back."

The older woman nodded even as the man cupped her elbow in a huge hand that warmed her entire body through her woolen jacket. The clicking of nails on the cement floor revealed a medium-sized dog of mixed heritage from behind the counter. Its tail wagged as the animal bounced in anticipation of going outside.

"Gizmo, stay," the man said.

Immediately the dog's tail dropped and he padded back to his bed.

"Yours?" Cobie asked the man as he led her out the double doors.

"Got him from the Pound." He waved to a bale of hay. "Take a seat and tell me how I can be of service to you."

Service? OMG! Her mind went straight to sex. Whether his remark was intentional or not, she had to focus for concentrating proved difficult with the innuendo.

She tried to keep her gaze fixed on his thick hair shinning under the winter sun. She thought it looked sort of sexy the way he tucked it behind his ears. She forced herself to stop having those thoughts. In her practical mind, business came first.

Marshaling herself, she glanced at the sky. Not a cloud in sight. The weatherman was wrong…again. They usually were in this part of the country. In all likelihood Yvonne would be pissed. Cobie wouldn't have been surprised if her friend secretly hoped for snow. She was always doing happy dances if flurries happened.

Cobie pulled her attention back to the tall man. "Join me," she offered, sitting down, patting the hay. A biting wind buffeted her, lifting jacket lapels. Spring might be around the corner, but winter was unwilling to give up its hold on the land. She wished she'd worn gloves.

He took a step, stopped, then fidgeted from foot to foot. "I prefer to stand."

Cobie could tell the man wanted to grill her, but kept a tight rein on his curiosity. Admirable. His willingness to listen without judgment raised her estimation of him higher. A good start in her opinion. If she could entice him with the idea of a new adventure, it might encourage him to sell his land.

"I don't bite," she said, licking her lips.

"Maybe I do," he answered her, casting a glance over fields tinted green.

Go for it big guy. I might enjoy being bit by you.

Cobie inhaled a calming breath after the crazy thought. Playing word games was a terrible sales technique. And she knew better.

She offered up a smile. "Promise me you'll hear me out before you make a decision."

****

Madden couldn't help frowning. The pretty woman looked cold, and he despised seeing anyone uncomfortable. Plus, he didn't like her assumption. It was a guess, and he hated speculating without all the facts. It wasn't how he functioned, but a weird tingle of excitement teased the back of his mind. He was dying to learn why the attractive woman patronized his store. Then the sight of moisture gleaming on full lips tinted pink threw him for a loop.

"I don't make promises I can't keep. Besides, my gut tells me it would be unwise to do so." He paused to survey the green rows less than twenty feet away. In a month the flowers would be in full bloom. "Can you explain in five words or less?"

Why the hell did he say that? It sounded like he was turning their conversation into a game. Which he wasn't!

"Make it ten," she countered with a twinkle in her pretty eyes.

He blinked. Her quick response surprised him. Carolyn would have had a hissy fit. It was always her way or the highway. Instinct shouted this woman was different. Nicer. "You're negotiating with me?"

She didn't answer. Instead a smile revealed movie star teeth gleaming snow-white and dazzling. "Seven words."

"Four," he said automatically.

Blue eyes that reminded him of a summer sky widened. "Hey, that's not fair. It's less than your original offer."

"You countered me. It's like poker. When you didn't call my bluff, the stakes change. You're the one who wanted to see me." For the life of him he didn't know why he was bargaining with this woman. He didn't know her. Probably would never see her again.

"I'll do it in three."

Surprise rippled through him. What could be explained in three words?

"Done." He stuck out his hand to seal the deal.

A chilly hand accepted his in a firm grip and she gave him one swift shake. "Deal."

He had the oddest urge to pull her close, but forced himself to step back and grin at her perched on the bale of hay. She reminded him of a male willow goldfinch, the Washington State bird. Sometimes the colorful bird populated the fields hunting for insects. "This ought to be short and sweet. You can start any time."

"Sell your property."

CHAPTER THREE

What the hell…

Cold, crisp air froze the soles of Madden's shoes to the parking lot. He fought through the shock of the woman's announcement, trying to assimilate her words. Hard to do with the world tilting on its axis.

Or was it because the sun had disappeared behind a bank of clouds?

"Who are you?" he asked.

She jumped to her feet. "I already told you— Cobie Brooks."

Insight hit on him with the force of a disc harrow plucking bulbs from the ground and he felt like a fool. He squeezed his eyes shut to calm his racing pulse before responding. "As in C. J. Brooks from Staple Construction?"

"One and the same. I thought you recognized my name when I introduced myself."

Madden didn't get angry. At least not easily. He took a deep breath. No one could make him sell his farm. "Get off my property."

He pointed to the parking lot where a single sports car sat. The black vehicle must belong to her. It fit her. Both were sleek, sharp, and sexy.

She hopped off the hay bale, stepping toward him and laying her hand on his arm, a tentative expression on her appealing face. "Let me explain!"

He took a step back, his ire peaking. Not at her. At himself because he felt himself weaken. Damn. What was wrong with him? Why was he vacillating? It wasn't like him at all.

A snowflake fluttered in the air. He looked skyward to see dark grey clouds roll in with the promise of a doozy of a winter storm.

****

The man was softening. He looked directly into her eyes, indicating interest. At least that was Cobie's interpretation of his body language. Scientists claimed sixty-five percent of communication came from facial expressions and body movements.

Or her imagination was playing tricks on her.

"Can we take this inside?" she asked, edging closer, blowing on her hands to warm them. "It's getting cold."

He covered his mouth, a sign of wanting to hide an emotional reaction. "Sure, but you're not changing my mind about selling."

That's what you think.

Cobie kept her delight hidden. A stubborn person was always easier to persuade than one who hadn't made up their mind. She could read people pretty good, and something about Madden Westerdahl told her he'd see through any flattery.

She started with her first impression. "I'm sure you're a reasonable man, Mr. Westerdahl. All I'm asking is for you to listen with an open mind."

"Why should I?"

She swallowed. "Just give me a chance."

"Five minutes is all I'll spare."

Plenty of time, she thought, as they walked in tandem to the door where a blast of heated air greeted them upon entering. The older woman at the cash register glanced in their direction, giving them a big smile.

The Shepherd mix stuck his head around the corner of the counter as if testing the atmosphere before rising. The man smiled at the dog, then nodded at the woman behind the counter before aiming a hard look in her direction.

Cobie didn't bother explaining. She had to figure out what would motivate him to sell. Better to stay calm herself and let him wait and wonder for a few seconds. Instead, she smiled at the clerk. "Save that vase for me."

"Susan, I'm taking my guest to the break room," the farm owner said. "Come get me if you need anything."

"Will do, boss. Want me to bring some coffee?"

Madden Westerdahl glanced at Cobie as if silently asking whether or not she wanted a cup. Someone raised the man right…with manners.

"Black. Please."

"Make it two cups, Susan," he responded.

He led her to a bare-bones room hardly larger than a broom closet with four chairs and a card-playing size table. A waste basket in the corner contained a crumbled bag from a fast-food hamburger shop. The faint greasy odor of fries lingered in the air.

"Sit down." The farmer took a seat kitty-corner from her. "First, tell me why I should waste my time listening to you?"

"That's easy. I'll be offering you a good deal."

A scowl didn't mar his good looks. "To sell land that's been in my family for over a hundred years. Not gonna happen."

"Mr. Westerdahl," she said instead of using his given name. "I understand the sentimentality attached to your farm, but if you agree to accept my company's offer, your land will provide hundreds of homes for others. Plus, the influx of people will boost the local economy."

"I already employee dozens of people and that helps the economy."

"Seasonal work. Right?"

She scored a direct hit if his frown was any indication. "My friends and neighbors like the status quo, and they might not appreciate an invasion of strangers who'll bring congestion to the roads and a burden on our services."

The man was no dummy. His assessment was correct. Cobie had grown up in a small town outside Phoenix and as the population mushroomed in the city, people moved into the outlining communities, changing them forevermore. "How can I convince you to do the right thing?"

"Right for you. Wrong for me." His silver grey gaze drilled into her.

She leaned back with a shiver that she couldn't tell whether it stemmed from dread or delight. "You don't know that unless you possess a crystal ball that predicts the future. There's no profit in the sale for me. I'm not on commission. I am on salary at Staple Construction."

"Hmmm."

The deep rumble from his wide chest triggered warmth to purl through her. Strange, but nice. She'd never felt such an instant attraction to a handsome man. She was a prosaic. In fact, her brain tried to distract her, almost understanding his reluctance to sell the family farm. *Almost.* Business was number one in her book. If she wanted to get into project management, she needed to remain focused.

"Does that mean you would consider an offer if I presented one?"

Those mesmerizing grey eyes narrowed. "I'm thinking this conversation is over."

Panic increased her heart rate. Before she could respond, a knock pounded on the door and Susan entered with two cups of aromatic coffee.

"I brought cookies, too," she said, beaming. "Enjoy."

Cobie accepted the cup and selected a peanut butter cookie, her favorite cookie her mom made. "Thanks, Susan," she said, meaning it.

The woman winked and left.

Cobie took her time tasting the coffee while ignoring the farmer's none-too-subtle suggestion about terminating their conversation. Wasn't going to happen. "What if I start with an actual offer?"

"If it means you'll go away faster."

Not exactly an enthusiastic beginning. Oh, well. Inhaling deeply, determined, she admitted, "I did a little investigation on land values and the going rate for vacant land is about five thousand dollars per acre. You have about four hundred acres. If my math is correct, you'd come out with millions. Plus, Staple is willing to throw in a bonus to sweeten the pot. Say another hundred thousand."

"It isn't always about money. This is my home, where I grew up."

If not money, what made this man tick? "It'll be a fair offer. There won't be any real estate commissions. No hidden fees." Silence greeted her proposal. Not what she expected. "Well, what do you think?"

The farmer stirred in his chair across from her. "I think you've wasted your time."

Okay. This wasn't how she planned their first meeting to go. Changing his mind was going to be an uphill climb on a slippery slope.

She visualized laying her cards on the table, explaining how a new development would benefit the community and free up his obligations.

Locking her gaze to his, she rose to the challenge. "Let me decide."

A few seconds later another knock rattled the door.

"Come in," the man said, looking over his shoulder.

Cobie liked the fact that he remained seated. An indication of his willingness to listen.

The female employee entered with the dog on her heels. "Hey, boss, it's starting to snow. I'm gonna leave early. Okay?"

"Go, Susan. I don't want John coming after me if you get stuck or have an accident."

Laughing, the older woman backed out of the room and shut the door with a click.

Cobie watched him break a cookie in half to feed the dog. The dog gulped the treat, then laid on the floor at the man's feet, head stretched to his lap.

The farmer turned to her, furrows on his brow. "Your five minutes are nearly up. Maybe you should hit the road too."

"Appreciate your concern, but I'm not afraid of a little snow."

"Suit yourself."

Cobie smiled to herself. She swore she was making progress.

****

Five minutes turned into an hour. Madden decided he'd been polite long enough. He'd been raised to let people speak, but he wasn't being fair, wasting the woman's time. No way was he interested in selling. When he stood, Gizmo jumped to his feet, tail wagging, eager for an adventure. "I've heard enough. I think you'd better leave."

Silence filled the small break room.

The woman stared at him, gorgeous blue eyes full of fire, without speaking for several seconds. Rising from her chair, she inhaled as if to gather strength. "I'm not quitting, Mr. Westerdahl."

"I am." He opened the door to indicate they leave. Gizmo stood beside him and stared back and forth at them.

An ominous quiet filled the store as he led the irritating woman through the aisles to the main entrance. Hold on a minute! To be fair she wasn't irritating. Her idea was. He actually liked talking to her.

Slowing, he cracked the main doors open. The air swirled with big, fat flakes. A captivating blanket of snow covered the world. At least four inches of snow had turned the landscape a glistening white.

Gizmo barged outside before Madden could stop him. The dog acted like a puppy, giving a good imitation of a jack rabbit as he leapt and bounced, snapping at falling snow.

"Someone enjoys snow," the woman said, disrupting his trance.

"This is a hell of a storm," he said. "It might not be safe for you to drive in this weather." Why'd he say that? What was the matter with him? He wanted to get rid of her.

"Watch me."

Stubborn woman. He was trying to warn her. "Don't get me wrong. I'm not telling you what to do. I've never seen snow come down this hard and fast, and I've lived here all my life. The roads are going to be a mess."

"It's not like I'm driving cross-country. I'm only going to Kirkland." She peered at him and a snowflake whirled inside the store to catch on the tips of her long eyelashes before melting. "Thanks for your concern, though. I'll be fine."

She turned and stomped across the parking lot. While he admired her long-legged strides, it only took seconds before she was slipping and sliding in the snow. His gut twisted. Half-way to her car her arms flew out to keep her center of gravity over her legs. Too little, too late.

Those good-looking legs shot out from under her and she went down hard on her right leg.

Gizmo stopped chasing snowflakes to race across the parking lot to the downed woman.

Madden raced toward her as well. "Gizmo, back. Are you all right?" he asked, pushing the dog away and slipping his hands under her arms to help her stand.

The instant she stood, she crumbled to the ground with a sharp cry of pain.

His heart raced. "What's wrong?"

Tears glistened in her eyes. "It's my ankle. I think it's broken."

"Let me check."

"No, no, that's unnecessary. Just help me to my car. I'll drive myself to an urgent care facility."

He shook his head, knowing he might regret his decision, but he'd face that later. "Listen... Trust me. There's no way you can drive any distance if your right ankle is screwed up."

"What do you suggest I do?"

"Let me take a look at your ankle. I know a little about first aid."

He didn't wait for permission. He called for Gizmo to follow him and scooped her up, amazed how well her slim body fit in his arms. It took no effort to carry her inside the store, sneaking peeks at a face contorted in agony.

What a mulish woman. She should have known better than stomping off on a slick surface in high heels. Surprisingly she didn't complain except for that first yelp. Carolyn would have screamed bloody murder and blamed him for the whole accident. The behavior was a pleasant change.

He found a chair and set the woman on it.

"Sorry about your shoe. I'll see if I can find the heel. Maybe you can have it repaired."

"Thanks, but don't worry about it."

He removed a heelless shoe and lifted her pant leg to reveal a long calf and ankle. Nice. A lot of men were boob guys, but he always went for legs—straight and slender were super sexy to him.

"Well," she said.

Snapping out of his wonder of her anatomy, he cupped her heel and held toes painted cobalt blue. Very gently he rotated her ankle. She compressed pink lips in an attempt to keep a moan from escaping.

He glanced up. "How do you feel?"

"It hurst."

"Not broken, but you'll need to get an x-ray in case there's a hair-line fracture. I don't think it's sprained. More likely you twisted it," he explained. "You probably will have bruising. Best to stay off it for a while."

He glanced out the window. Large snowflakes continued to fall. Already, their steps and all trace of Gizmo's antics in the parking lot were covered up.

"Maybe I can drive to a motel and get a room. There's got to be one along the freeway."

"There's a couple close by. Simple way to find out is to call first...to make sure they've got rooms. If they do, I'll drive you over. Meanwhile, sit there and I'll check."

She offered a half-grimace, half-smile. "Thanks much."

He went to the cash register and pulled out a dog-eared phone book from under the counter. The first number answered after several rings and went to a recording stating that they had no vacancies. The next motel was a bit farther, but worth a try. It was answered on the second ring.

"Pit Stop Motel," said a young sounding voice. "How may I help you?"

He smiled at Cobie. "Do you have any rooms available tonight?"

"I'm sorry the last room was booked an hour ago. Have you tried Travel Express?"

"All ready did. Thanks." He pushed the end button on his cell phone, wondering what he was going to do with an injured woman on his hands. She looked up at him as if he could solve the world's problems and he felt himself melt into blue eyes that would make the perfect tulip color.

"No luck? What am I supposed to do?"

A very good question.

"Looks like you're stuck with me for a while."

CHAPTER FOUR

No way was she staying with the handsome farmer.

Her libido couldn't handle being in close proximity with him. He was a far too tempting specimen of male deliciousness. She'd seen too many women give up their careers after falling in love. That wasn't going to happen to her. "Thanks for the offer, but maybe I'll just stay in my car until the throbbing stops."

"Don't be silly. It's freezing outside and by the looks of those clouds, the weather isn't going to improve any time soon. I have ibuprofen at my house that'll take the edge off your pain. You should elevate your foot to keep the swelling down. My sister broke her leg once, her crutches might still be in her bedroom. I'll look when we get inside. I can put on a pot of coffee and throw a late lunch, early dinner together for us while you figure out what to do. We can catch the weather report on TV. Sound good?"

"Better than good. I really appreciate your hospitality."

She was hurting and hungry, having skipped breakfast. His suggestion made sense and two people knew she was here—that older female employee and Yvonne. She didn't know about the employee, but Yvonne was a pit bull and would turn the world upside down to find her. Besides, because their jobs took them all around the Puget Sound, they shared a Find Me app on their phones. Cobie's confidence rose. She should be safe with the farmer.

Was he safe from her?

Where'd that come from? Stupid thoughts belonged to stupid people, which she didn't consider herself one.

He chuckled. "You haven't tasted my cooking. And the offer's only good if we don't talk about selling my farm."

The sound of his deep voice felt like fingers tickling her spine. "I can always lend a hand."

"A one-legged helper. That ought to be worth seeing." He scooped her up in his arms without another word. "Let's go. It's only a hundred feet between the store and my place. Gizmo, come."

Cobie's breath hitched at the contact. The muscles in his arms bulged from hard work. Nothing soft about this man. Up close, his after shave flooded her nose with hints of a summery breeze and a light licorice scent. If she were honest with herself, he smelled good enough to eat.

Stop that! He was a business deal. Nothing more, nothing less.

After an embarrassing but pleasant jaunt in the man's arms, a genuine farm house built in another century loomed before her. "Put me down. I can walk the rest of the way on my own."

The dog raced up the steps to pace before the door on a wrap-around porch.

"No! You need to keep weight off that leg." So saying, the farmer tightened his hold and dashed up the stairs with her cradled in his arms. "Remember you've only got one leg and you fell with two. Once inside, I'll find those crutches."

Her eyes widened with amazement when they entered what she anticipated would be a house smelling of years of use without modern improvements. She couldn't have been farther from the truth. The interior boasted an open floor plan with an abundance of natural light, neutral grey walls with touches of royal blue and white in the furniture and paintings, mostly of tulip fields in full bloom. She loved it on sight.

True to his word, the farmer set her down on a dark navy sofa with wooden arms and pillows embroidered with tulips. She recognized it as Stickley, a Mission style of sturdy oak furniture that became popular in the 1900s. Expensive furniture. Her grandmother had owned a chair with similar arms, although Cobie estimated this furniture was much newer.

Were her sources wrong about his financial troubles? There was money somewhere in the Westerdahl family. No wonder he wasn't interested in selling. He didn't need the money.

"Not what I expected," she said, wiping her hand over the corduroy fabric.

Gizmo padded over to her and laid his head on her lap. She scratched behind his ears. Her effort brought several licks or kisses as a reward. So like the dogs she'd owned as a kid.

The farmer grinned. "Fooled you, huh? Just because I live in a ninety-year-old house doesn't mean it wouldn't be updated along the way. My mom and dad had the place remodeled about ten years ago."

"Sorry. I wasn't being critical. Kudos to your parents for doing a wonderful job."

"Oh. Mom always appreciates compliments." A look of relief passed over his face as he spoke over his shoulder. "I'll get that ice pack and the ibuprofen. Between the two, they should take the edge off and help keep the swelling down. Use the pillows to elevate your leg."

"Thanks."

A minute later he returned and gently placed an ice pack on her ankle. She sucked in a breath.

"You okay?"

"Fine. Just have to get used to the cold."

He nodded. "I'll fix that pot of coffee. The remote's on the coffee table in front of you. Turn on TV and we'll catch the weather."

She glanced where he directed and spotted the remote on a long wooden table, another Stickley piece. She clicked on the TV. All stations were broadcasting special reports of the winter storm. She selected her favorite channel. The lead weatherwoman stood before a map of Washington State. Every city shown on the screen had numbers indicating snow accumulations.

The weatherwoman smiled at the camera. "This storm is a genuine blizzard and should break the 1950 record of 63 inches. If you don't have to drive, please stay off the roads. Two to four inches of snow is coming down every hour and is predicated to continue throughout the night and into tomorrow."

"Well that sucks. Even if I could drive, it wouldn't be safe. A couple years ago we had a few inches and I got stuck in my car Black Beauty, BB for short," she went on seeing confusion appear on his face. "My co-worker's brother thought it was my lack of experience in driving in snow. He went down with a friend to bring BB home and couldn't get it unstuck. I had to wait for the roads to clear."

The farmer came around the sofa with two cups of coffee. "Weather is fickle in these parts. It could reach sixty degrees in a few days. You just never know. Last year we had two days in the seventies in January. In the meantime, since we might be together for a while, let's start over. Call me Madden."

She accepted the coffee. Deep down, she didn't object to spending time with the handsome farmer. He was more than he appeared and she was eager to delve into the bottom of the mystery. "Thanks, Madden."

He smiled when she used his name. The haunted look that seemed a permanent fixture vanished and his face transformed in something superior…again. Cobie's toes curled.

"No problem. I did promise you lunch." He glanced at the flat screen on the wall. "It's going to take time for things to return to normal. Glad I stocked up the other day."

"The freeway should clear by tomorrow. It'll be the weekend. Less traffic."

"It's no inconvenience. It'll be nice to have company. Do you play cribbage?"

"My dad taught me when I was a teenager. He learned in the Navy."

"Mine was in the Navy, too. I was five when I first learned, so fair warning, I'm a pretty good player." He scooted forward. "Where was your dad stationed?"

"Dad was at the Inactive Service Craft Facilities in Hawaii. He hated being stationed there. Said he didn't like being land-locked. Mom could only get him to visit once after they were married. Yours?"

"The Alabama, a missile submarine, stationed in Bangor."

"Washington?"

"Yep. He joined the Navy to see the world, went to A-school in San Diego, then to his disappointment was stationed on the Alabama. My grandparents were happy to have him so close."

Grinning at the tiny thread weaving around her heart that both their fathers were in the Navy, she was glad they shared a common thread. "I doubt I'll be much competition with cribbage. I haven't played in years. And if I'm going to call you Madden, you must call me Cobie."

"Great. I'll start a fire, fix lunch, and we can play for penny a point or toothpicks."

Cobie swore a teasing note laced his deep voice and she loved the easy camaraderie. Her tulip farmer was much easier to like now that he wasn't ordering her off his property.

****

Too pretty for her own good.

That's what Madden decided when he tried to dismiss the reason for Cobie's visit.

It was more pleasurable focusing on her classic features that were a photographer's wet dream. It had been ages since he found a woman distractingly attractive—too busy working the farm, forging a profitable business out of the hole his parents had dug. Not that he blamed them. The tulip market had been dropping for years and no one really noticed until the bottom fell away.

He got the fire crackling, letting heat blast the living room.

He poured food in Gizmo's bowl, tossed a couple ice cubes into his water dish, then fixed tuna sandwiches with potato chips and carried the food and glasses of ice water on a tray into the living room. He used the old-fashioned shaped tulips ones his mother had purchased in an antique store. "I brought the cribbage board and cards too. Plus, some socks and slippers for you. They're probably too big, but cold feet aren't any fun."

With a polite smile, Cobie accepted the plate. He had placed a bottle of ibuprofen on the tray. She opened the bottle and washed down a couple pills with a swallow. Then she put on the over-sized socks and slippers with a laugh. "Oh, this feels heavenly."

"I'm glad you're happy," he said, realizing he meant it.

When she opened the sandwich and layered chips onto the bread all he could do was stare in fascination.

"What?" she asked, looking up.

He didn't answer immediately, just did the same with his sandwich, squished the mass together, took a bite, then pointed to his full mouth. They shared a similar taste in food. Swallowing, he grinned. "My favorite way to eat tuna fish."

"Normally, I like chips with ridges, but these'll do in an emergency." She winked as she picked up the cards and shuffled. "Ready to see who is best at this game?"

"You're on."

Setting his sandwich on his plate, he rubbed his hands together. Nothing like an appealing opponent to give him a challenge. The day was certainly turning into an interesting one.

They left the TV on low to check on the blizzard. By all accounts another storm might roll in a day or so after the current one ended.

Bad for businesses, except tow trucks and hotels.

Gizmo trotted into the living room and climbed on the sofa to curl next to Cobie's side.

After four games with each winning two, they went for the tie breaker. Carolyn disliked playing card games. Maybe because she usually exaggerated her skills and pouted when she lost. He liked the fact that this woman wasn't a braggart.

"What time is it?" Cobie asked, stifling yawn.

A soft glow from the fireplace reflected off her smooth skin. He found himself admiring the symmetry of her heart-shaped face. A wide forehead, high cheeks, and the blue of her eyes deepened as night fell. All attractive features.

He dealt six cards to each of them, immediately tossing two into the crib. "Late. We'd better make this the last hand. You can take my sister's old bedroom. I think she even left a set of pjs in the dresser. You're welcome to use whatever you find."

"Thanks." She glanced at the board as she discarded two cards in to the crib. "If we quit before the game is over the person ahead is called the winner."

Much to his surprise he found this time with Cobie entertaining and hated to see the evening end, but rest would help her heal faster.

He glanced at the pegs on the board. The last hand put him on home-street and the chance of skunking her loomed as a real possibility. "I'm ahead right now. Want to concede?"

"Not gonna happen, smarty-pants. You'd like that wouldn't you? I get to count first and could get a twenty hand."

He loved the teasing lilt in her voice. "Go for it."

CHAPTER FIVE

Cobie woke in a strange bedroom with her ankle throbbing, and the air redolent with the scent of bacon and coffee. Her stomach growled. Yesterday's sandwich and chips had been her only meal and now her body reacted to the delicious aroma of food.

Swinging her legs off the bed and putting weight on her feet, she nearly collapsed from shooting pain. Stars exploded in her eyes. Her ankle was killing her. She gritted her teeth and leaned over to examine it. Swollen, ugly with dark purpling encircling her ankle. She might have only twisted it, but it hurt like hell. Shaking her head, she grabbed the crutches Madden found for her.

The drapes were closed and, in an act of defiance, she refused to look outside to check how deep the snow accumulation. Stripping off the flannel pjs with flying pigs, she tossed on her wool slacks and blouse. No need for the matching jacket. Her feet swam in the white socks and brown slippers, but did their job and kept her feet warm.

Making her way into the kitchen became the hardest thing she'd done in her life. She wasn't the most coordinated person, but determination saw her through the ordeal. Moving required placing the crutches a short distance in front her and swinging her body forward as she moved.

Madden stood at the stove, bacon sizzling in a pan. Dressed in jeans and a dark grey T-shirt that made his eye-color pop, his movements appeared effortless and for some strange reason she found watching him heart-skipping appealing.

Damn. She shouldn't have those kinds of thoughts. This was business, not developing a relationship.

Gizmo rose to greet her, tailing wagging.

Two place settings on tulip placemats were arranged on the kitchen island. A vase of glass tulips that she hadn't noticed before was tucked in the corner near the fridge. Tulips images were sprinkled everywhere through the house. Smiling to herself, she leaned the crutches against the counter, slipped onto a stool, glad to be off her foot. A steaming cup of coffee wafted its intoxicating scent in the air. An ibuprofen bottle sat next to the cup. What a thoughtful man. "I hope this is mine."

"Sure is. I heard you moving about and figured you'd need something to feed your soul."

"Coffee in the morning is the elixir of the gods as far as I'm concerned."

He placed bacon on a plate with a paper towel under the strips. "Protein to keep you healthy. Eggs will be up in a jiffy."

"You don't need to go to all this trouble."

"You're my guest. How's your ankle?"

"Not good. It hurts to put weight on it." She lifted the ibuprofen bottle in the air. "Thanks for these."

Toast popped out of a toaster. Madden grabbed the slices and slathered butter on them. With his back toward her, the cotton fabric stretched from his movements giving her the opportunity to ogle his broad shoulders and narrow waist. His thick hair was slightly tossed as if he'd just ran fingers through it to straighten the tangles of sleep. Nothing wrong in admiring a fine specimen of manhood.

Turning around, he slipped a plate of toast and eggs under her nose. "You're probably starved. Eat."

Her nose inhaled the comforting aroma of toast and butter and her mouth watered. "Thanks. It smells delicious."

"You're welcome. Breakfast is the most important meal of the day. It fuels you up and gets you ready for the day. I'm used to fixing myself a hearty meal before I start my day."

She traced a finger on the edges of the tulip on her placement. "Tell me about tulips."

Madden settled in the stool next to her. He broke off a piece of toast and fed Gizmo sitting at his feet. "There are about seventy-five species of tulips. I bet you didn't know they were originally a wild flower in Turkey."

She sipped her coffee. "No, I didn't."

"A few things you might not know about tulips is the word is actually a corruption of a Turkish word, *tülbent*, meaning gauze or muslin—which is derived from the Persian word *delband*, meaning turban. It was a tradition to wear the flower in one's turban. They were introduced into Europe via diplomats of the day and became a frenzied commodity."

She enjoyed hearing him talk. His voice was deep, smooth and just plain sexy. "Wasn't it in the sixteenth or seventeenth century that there was something of a Tulip mania or tulip craze? I read the cost of a single bulb of a new variety was acceptable as a dowry for a bride."

"I'm impressed. The craze reached its height in Holland between 1633-37. The trade was restricted to professional growers and experts, but the growing prices tempted many, ordinary middle-class and poorer families to speculate in the tulip market. The market became volatile and crashed in early 1637."

"Sounds like today's stock market."

"It wasn't as bad as history reports. According to historian, Anne Goldgar, not a single person went bankrupt. Even Dutch painter van Goyen, who allegedly lost everything in the tulip crash, lost his fortune in land speculation. The craze came to an end, but the flowers remained fashionable. Today, they're called jewel in the garden and I couldn't agree more." He stopped to shovel eggs on his toast. Swallowing, he grinned at her. "I can be an encyclopedia when it comes to tulips. Want more information?"

She flicked her gaze out the kitchen window. Her mouth dropped. Beyond there weren't inches of snow—but feet. Part of her spirits sank. She'd never get out of here. Another part trembled with delight. She was trapped with Madden.

Not such a bad predicament.

"I think I have time on my hands," she said, crunching on crispy bacon cooked just the way she liked it.

He followed her gaze. "Yeah. It's going to be a while before anyone ventures anywhere." He shrugged. "Closer to home… The very first person to grow tulips in Washington State was George Gibbs, an immigrant from England in the early nineteen hundreds. He found success growing the bulbs and others followed in his steps. In nineteen forty-six, William Roozen arrived in the United States. He bounced around working on different tulip farms, but in nineteen fifty-five he purchased the Washington Bulb Company, making him the leader among the flower-growing families in Skagit Valley. The farm operates a public display garden and has a gift shop called Roozengaarde, which alongside the DeGoede family's Tulip Town are major attractions during the Tulip Festival. I'm small potatoes compared to them."

A modest man. She recalled the female employee boasting that this farm was the best source for tulips. She wondered which version was true. More likely, somewhere in the middle.

Eating her fill, she was contented…more than contented to listen to Madden's deep voice weave its magic as he relayed the history of tulips in Skagit Valley. "If I did my homework correctly, the tulip festival started in the eighties."

"As a three-day event to increase revenue to the area. Mt. Vernon started as a logging town, but when the mills closed…" His voice trailed off. "The town was dying. Council members had to become creative, so they came up with the tulip festival. It has since grown to a month-long event and coincides with street fairs, art shows, and sporting events. Over a million visitors come during the festival."

Sounded like a perfect lead in to her. "So, the whole area benefits from the festival. Wouldn't it be nice if the residents didn't have to depend on such a narrow window to make ends meet? A new housing development could bring year-long revenue into the area."

The atmosphere in the cozy kitchen turned chillier than outdoors.

Madden stood abruptly. "You done?"

Cobie wished she'd bitten her tongue. She'd turned a pleasant moment into something awful. "You cooked. I'll clean up."

"Thanks, but no thanks." He began picking up the dirty plates. "You can barely stand on your foot. You need to keep it elevated. By the looks outside, it'll be days before plows clear the streets, even the freeways. Hunker down and enjoy the winter wonderland."

When he returned from the sink, he stood over her offering his arm. She glanced at the crutches. Who was she to refuse a handsome man's arm? Easing herself off the stool, she leaned into him, never wanting the contact to end.

****

Why'd she have to mention the farm and selling in the same breath?

Madden's good mood evaporated in the blink of an eye. Cobie had ruined the moment.

It wasn't just her single-minded determination to buy property that had been in his family for three generations. He'd been impressed with her knowledge and when he helped her to the sofa, a soft breast had pushed against his arm and sent his horniness into over-drive. Damn woman had no business mucking up his life.

He watched Gizmo climb on the sofa and snuggle next to her. Traitor.

"I'm going to my workshop," he announced sharply. Maybe too sharply.

A crushed expression passed over Cobie's heart-shaped face before she managed to control it. "You're leaving me alone in your house?"

"The workshop's in the basement. I doubt you'll abscond with anything valuable. At least nothing heavy. If you need something, just holler. I'll hear you."

"I'm perfectly capable of taking care of myself." She turned her back on him and clicked on the TV.

His desertion hurt her feelings, and in turn, he was being dismissed. Fine with him. The less interaction with the woman, the better for him. He didn't need her company.

A big, fat lie.

He'd enjoyed cooking for Cobie, sharing the morning, explaining about tulips and the beginning of the business in Skagit Valley. He could see himself telling her about his plans for the day, every day. Why'd she have to destroy the ambience by bringing up the ugly business of selling the farm?

He stomped downstairs to where his grandfather had jerry-rigged a greenhouse to work on developing new tulips species. It wasn't difficult work. Nature had provided a head start. Tulips incredible variety had created unique colors, shapes and sizes—all beautiful in their own right.

Three generations of Westerdahls had sought to improve the flowers. A monumental task for a small farm, and one he believed himself capable of achieving and putting his own stamp on.

If he had enough time.

He puttered around, checking plants, lights, CO_2 levels, and controls, letting time slip by and his frustration mellow. He selected genetic material from flowers in last year's crop to hybridize. Tense muscles relaxed as he dug fingers into the soil and he planted newly formed seeds in small crates in the workshop under lights.

"I'm sorry I upset you."

He jumped, startled at hearing Cobie's voice less than ten feet away on the stairs. "What are you doing down here?"

"I got bored with TV. They keep repeating the same news over and over." She scanned the area, lifting her nose slightly. "So, it's true tulips have a slight honey aroma. I can just catch a hint with the damp soil."

Damn woman was too cute for her own good. And her comment only confirmed his impression that she knew her stuff. "How'd you get down here without me hearing you?"

"If you must know I scooted on the steps via my bottom. I didn't mean to startle you." Her gaze swept over the basement turned into greenhouse, widening ever so slightly at the number of free-standing shelves with shallow bins lining the walls, each with a year and picture of nucleus bulbs on them. "I would never have guessed this was down here."

"My grandfather couldn't afford to build a commercial greenhouse. He needed a place to work when he started tweaking his tulip crop and NeMa knew he had a dream. It took him seven years to develop his first species—the Allsip—a pink tulip with red tips, NeMa's maiden name."

"Seven years?"

Her tone revealed interest, so he explained, "In the first year, no flower appears. The plant produces only leaves to grow and strengthen the bulb. The process is repeated for five to seven years, never knowing what the end flower will look like. It's more scientific than it appears."

"Explain to a dummy."

He seriously doubted the accuracy of her statement. "Once the new flower emerges, healthy and robust, the work goes on. The bulb offshoots have to reach maturity and each new bulb has to multiply to turn a single flower into thousands. That process can add another ten to fifteen years before ready for sale. Grampa's took another ten years to make commercially viable. Luckily, it was an instant hit with tulip lovers. Dad followed in his footsteps. You were looking at his lime creation in the retail store. He started them when he was in his early twenties and we just put them on the market a couple years ago."

"Now, it's your turn," she said.

The smile Cobie aimed at him heated his insides toasty warm. "Yep. I was born to grow tulips. Those over there are ones I started in high school. I should see flowers on some this year." He couldn't keep pride out of his voice as he glanced at stalks with flower buds ready to bloom. "It takes faith to be a bulb developer."

"And patience, I'd say." She leaned against the railing and frowned as though trying to grasp the information he had shared. "But why does it take so long?"

"That's the nature of the plant. There's tons of work behind every species."

She glanced around the basement a second time, taking in the dozens of bins. "So, this represents decades of work. Like research all the pharmaceutical companies have to do to develop a new drug. I never realized growing flowers could be as complicated."

Her interest seemed sincere and he did love his work. "Fingers are always crossed that it will appeal to the fickle tulip lovers of the world. All a farmer can hope is that the new flower stands out."

"What do you hope to achieve?" She hopped on one foot to sit on a stool he kept near the bench.

The urge to rush to her aid swelled, but she hopped like a wild rabbit and reached the stool before he could act. "With the tulips?"

"Uh huh."

"That should be obvious—a commercial success."

She fingered the potting soil in the bin on the workbench. "I get a feeling there's more."

Damn. She called him on his dream, and for some unexplainable reason he wanted her to understand. He lost himself in the depth of her blue eyes, then shook free. "Oh, all right. Tulip flowers come in a multitude of colors, except pure blue. Several have 'blue' names but they only have a faint violet hue. I'm after that pure blue."

Her eyes widened. "After centuries of people trying to achieve it, is it really possible?"

"I'm staking my future on it. Westerdahls name their flowers after family members, so they'll live on forever. It's a tradition I intend to continue."

"Commitment takes dedication. Hard work."

He didn't need a reminder. What she said was ingrained in his blood. "Tell me about it."

"Besides this elusive blue flower, what's the most popular?"

The glint in Cobie's eyes delighted him. "Depends on the individual. Tulips are members of the lily family. You can enjoy the flowers from March through May. A flower with perfect blooms is considered highly desirable. Red is probably the most popular, but people like different, too. The Angelique is considered one of the most beautiful. It bears classic feminine, double, soft pink flowers that look like peonies."

"Guess I'm a neophyte when it comes to growing tulips."

"Oh, I think you know a lot more about tulips than you're letting on."

CHAPTER SIX

"Guilty as charged," Cobie answered, enjoying the time sitting in the basement with Madden, surrounded by generations of hard work.

His expression hardened the tiniest bit. "Thought so."

"The best way to understand a potential client is to learn how they tick. I don't mean personal information. I read up on tulips a bit. Now I know just enough to be dangerous," she said, wanting him to understand.

"Oh, you're dangerous alright." A small smile lifted the corners of his luscious-looking mouth.

She swore he appreciated her honesty and willingness to research before approaching him. "What's that supposed to mean?"

"Nothing. Just forget I said anything."

No wonder he baulked at selling his farm. Few people possessed his dedication and devotion. Cobie suspected quitting would be impossible for him. He should be admired. She sighed, understanding making her regret pressuring him.

Only one other person had expressed a similar passion—her Grandmother Mildred. She'd owned a small neighborhood grocery store before the big chains came into existence. It had been her heart and joy. As a kid, Cobie loved going to the store and running down the aisles. It broke both their hearts when the store had to close.

"You love this work, don't you?" she asked, pushing the sad memory into the recesses of her mind.

Madden wiped his dirty hands on a towel. "Yep. Like I said, I hope to continue creating and improving these tulips for the enjoyment of the world."

"Snow won't hurt the bulbs, will it?"

"They can handle short cold snaps without much of a problem. It's the freezing and thawing that tends to heave and shift the bulbs, pushing them toward the surface. This is really our first hard freeze. If the snow had come later, even two or three weeks, the biggest danger is when the flower buds form. After the flowers bloom, a late snow storm will cause brown spots on the petals. Even if the flower is damaged, the bulbs will be fine and come back year after year." He glanced at the steps leading upstairs. "Heard enough?"

Madden Westerdahl came across as a nice man trying to make it in a business better suited for the massive farms of Holland. Her instincts to root for the underdog soared. All Grandmother Mildred had needed was a helping hand and she might have weathered the economic changes. The same could be true for Madden. She hadn't been old enough to help her grandmother, but what if she could help him save his dream? It could balance the cosmic scales. Her breath caught in her throat.

Where'd that crazy thought come from?

She needed this deal. She'd already shown her company that she was good at marketing. Time to show them a new side. Otherwise, her chances of proving herself in this new field were slim to none.

Still, a question lingered. "Besides an influx of cash, what would it take to make your farm prosperous?"

Madden frowned. "Why do you care?"

She didn't blame him for becoming suspicious. They hadn't started off on the best of terms. "I'm interested. Talk to me? Tell me."

"Let's take this upstairs." He approached her; arms outstretched.

She leaned back on the stool. "Are you kidding? You're not carrying me up those stairs. You were lucky on the porch. But these are a heck of a lot higher. I can already visualize our broken bodies if we both fell."

"How do you propose to climb them?" A slight grin tugged at the corners of his mouth as he tucked an errant blond lock behind his ear.

Cobie averted her gaze. The sight of his upturned lips made her want to trace her fingers over them to feel the heat they generated. "The same way I got down here—by the power of my gluts."

"Well-defined gluts, I might add."

A rush of blood burned her cheeks at his remark. "Thanks, I think."

"I shouldn't have said that." So saying, he flashed a huge smile that transformed his whole face and lit up the room. "But I'm glad I did. Nor am I leaving you down here to climb up by yourself. If you won't let me carry you, I'll keep you company. That way if you tumble down, we go together."

"Don't be ridiculous."

"I'm not...I—" He clamped that luscious mouth of his shut.

Cobie didn't wait for him to finish. She hopped to the bottom steps, sat, and using her good leg started to push herself up one step at a time.

****

Madden couldn't stop grinning as he followed Cobie up the stairs on her magnificent gluteus maximus. "You sure you don't want my help?"

"Positive," she huffed. "Now let me concentrate."

"As you wish, but if I carried you, we'd get to the top much quicker."

"Go, I'm not stopping you."

The dirty look Cobie shot in his direction actually tickled him. She had such an expressive face. He bet she'd never make a good poker player.

When she reached the landing, he leapt over her and scooped her in to his arms to make it easier for her to grab the crutches leaning against the wall. He held her steady while she adjusted her arms for a comfortable fit. The extra seconds of wrapping his hands around her waist made him never want to let her go.

Yeah, right.

His hands felt empty when she hobbled to the sofa.

Gizmo stopped to sniff his food dish. A few crumbs from morning remained.

"How about I fix us some hot chocolate?"

"I don't want to be a bother."

"I'm enjoying myself."

"You're spoiling me," she said, settling on the sofa with a huff and using pillows to elevate her leg.

Gizmo joined her and curled up on the far cushion.

Ten minutes later he handed her a cup of cocoa with miniature marshmallows floating on top, letting his fingers brush hers. A tingle raced up his arm and he wondered if she experienced the same sensation.

"Anything on TV?" He nodded toward the screen, then glanced at the sofa where the only open spot was next to Cobie. It was a bad idea to sit near her. She was proving far too tempting for his sanity or peace-of-mind. If only she was someone he could trust completely. He genuinely wanted to believe she was interested in what he did, not just buy the farm.

"Same old thing. Join me," she said as if reading his mind, patting the cushion next to her.

He scowled at Gizmo. "He's got my spot. I should make him get off."

"Leave him alone. My dogs always sat with us when I was growing up."

"And where was that?" he asked, complying, and savoring the heat of her body reaching out to caress his thigh.

****

Cobie sipped the sweetened drink before answering, "Arizona. A small town called El Mirage. Snow birders swell the population during the winter months, but its shrinks in the summer."

She watched Madden nod and drink his hot chocolate. A brown line left a mark above his upper lip. The sight nearly did her in. He looked like a little boy in that marvelous body. She was tempted to lean over and brush a kiss over his mouth increased tenfold.

"Hmm. Good," he said, smiling, unaware of his effect on her.

"Yes, it is."

Her ringing cell phone stopped her from acting on the fantasy. Filled with disappointment, she glanced at the read out. Her assumption that Yvonne would keep an eye on her whereabouts proved accurate. "Excuse me. It's a co-worker. I better take it." At his nod, she hit the accept button. "Hello."

"Where are you? I left a voice mail on your phone, but you didn't respond. I worried about you all night."

Cobie nearly laughed. The sound must have disturbed Gizmo, for he jumped down and trotted to the kitchen. Madden moved over and claimed the dog's spot. "I'm fine. Did you check your Find Me app? I'm still in Mount Vernon."

"I know. I looked at it. You got a motel. Good for you."

Cobie pursed her lips together. "Hmmm, not exactly."

"You didn't spend the night in your car, did you? I'll have Ronnie come get you. He won't mind coming to your rescue. He lived in Tahoe for several years and knows how to drive in snow."

Cobie's heartrate increased. "No, no. I don't need to be rescued. That's too much to ask."

"Don't be silly. You know my brother's sweet on you?"

"I'm fine. Snug as a bug in a rug." It dawned on her as she spoke that she meant every word. The feelings she felt went against everything she thought she wanted most in the world.

"Where are you?"

Dare she tell? "I'm at the tulip farm. The owner kindly offered me his sister's empty room."

"You're alone with a stranger? That takes guts, girlfriend. I hope you know what you're doing."

Cobie didn't reply immediately. Inhaling deeply, she answered honestly, "Me too. I'll keep you posted and…and thanks for checking on me."

She pushed the end button on her cell.

Madden arched a brow. "Someone worried about you. Is this co-worker a boyfriend?"

"No, Yvonne is a female friend."

"Do you have a boyfriend?"

A definite twist on the conversation. He leaned close enough for her to inhale the light fragrance of his aftershave. This time it was something with the hint of fresh citrus and woodsy cedar. Her heart skipped. "I think we've gotten off-track. I'm here to convince you to sell your property to Staple Construction."

"I know, but I like this exchange better."

So did she.

CHAPTER SEVEN

Cobie never answered him about having a boyfriend.

Madden wondered if the omission had been intentional. Heat still lingered in his palms from holding her. It allowed him to speculate on the possibility of a future with Cobie.

The crazy thought came out of left field and threw him for a loop.

Madden kept his gaze riveted on her. Only the instant blush on her cheeks gave away her reaction to asking about a boyfriend. His confidence mounted that he could affect her. Maybe he did have a chance to start a romantic bond.

Nails clicked on wooden floors. Gizmo trotted into the living room and climbed up on the sofa to settle in the empty space between them. Clearly, the dog never heard the phrase that three's a crowd.

Cobie turned up the volume on the TV. A smiling weatherman was giving the seven-day weather and sure enough the forecast had changed...again. Instead of another storm, temperatures were predicated to rise to an unseasonable high. The snow would melt fast, causing flooding in all the familiar places.

And Cobie would leave.

"Looks like I'll be out of your hair within a day or so," she said.

The simple words upset his plans. Disappointment along with a sense of loss astonished him. "There's no rush. What's another day or so? If you must know, I've enjoyed your company. Never realized how empty my house was without someone to share it."

Cobie's blue eyes widened. "Are you asking me to stay?"

"I—I..." His voice trailed off, his tongue twisting in his mouth. What was the matter with him? That was exactly what he wanted her to do.

She laughed softly. "Stop worrying, Madden. I'm only teasing."

He wasn't. He had been serious.

Or, maybe confused. He'd never experienced feelings like he did around Cobie.

The idea of her remaining on a permanent basis appealed more than he imagined. "Guess I over-reacted... About everything."

"Hey, don't worry about it."

Except he was worried. What if he never saw her again?

Gizmo raised his head to stare at them. He patted the dog.

Cobie angled her head, swaying her silky bob. "If you don't mind me asking, why are you in this big house all by yourself? Where's your family?"

"Mom and Dad are in Australia visiting some friends. It's summer down there. They left after the holidays and will be home early spring. They'll bunk with me for a couple weeks and help during the festival, then it's off on a three/four-month cruise around the world."

The surprise on her face delighted him. "Where are they going? I mean, you said around the world."

"Their itinerary has them flying to Amsterdam to catch the cruise ship that's going to take them to England, along Portugal's coast, and down toward Africa. There's only two places I'm concerned about: the Somali Coast and the Gulf of Aden."

"Pirates?"

Her quick response didn't surprise him. It didn't take a genius to establish the pretty package that was Cobie Brooks held an even smarter brain. "When they first mentioned their trip, I researched it. Supposedly, piracy has slowed a bit in recent years. Oh, there's hot zones all around the world. The good news is that now cruise lines take preparations for all the scenarios and claim to be well-equipped to handle situations. There have only been six reported incidents of pirates attempting to attack cruise ships in recent years."

Cobie scooted forward. "Friends of my parents went a couple years ago. They were ordered to stay in their cabins while traveling in the dangerous waters. They said armed soldiers were brought on board to patrol the decks, and they convoyed with other cruise ships at full speed. Afterwards, the soldiers departed and the other ships went their separate ways."

"That's encouraging." While Cobie's news assuaged some of his worries, remnants lingered. They were his parents, after all.

"I didn't mean to worry you," she said, as if she caught his concern and genuinely cared. "I'm sure they'll be perfectly safe. My parents' friends said they had a once-in-a-lifetime trip."

He freed a sigh, savoring the encouragement. "They deserve their trips. They stayed home, never taking a vacation for decades. Dad focused on the farm. Being a tulip farmer isn't much different from any other farmer—dairy, wheat, etc. We're all the same. Animals and crops come first, but Mom invested in the stock market. She bought techie companies—Microsoft, Amazon, Google, and Facebook at the beginning when they were low."

"Wow."

"That's putting it mildly. I've got a smart mother."

"Sounds like it. I'm impressed with everything…and everyone I've seen." Cobie pursed her lips as if more questions formed.

He could only guess at their nature, and decided an open and honest discussion would strengthen their rapport. "They set up a trust for me, but I won't touch it. It's their money. They earned it, let them spend it. They're having a blast in Australia, seeing things they only saw on TV. Traveling was their dream and I don't begrudge them at all."

"You're a nice son," Cobie replied.

Warmth burst inside him. The praise on her lips made his heart swell with joy and he grinned.

****

Cobie adored his smile. She just loved the way it changed his appearance. "I'm sure they'll have lots to tell you." She glanced around the room; positive the homey touches came from his mother's hand. "What about your sister? Do you have just the one?"

Madden shrugged those wide shoulders of his. "Only one. Laura's older by eight years. She lives across the valley with her husband. They've got four kids which keeps her busy. I'm the last Westerdahl in the valley. End of the line...unless I find a woman willing to become a tulip farmer's wife and have kids with me."

A kaleidoscope of butterflies flew erratically in her stomach. Nervous laughter spilled out of Cobie. At twenty-eight, sometimes her biological clock ticked so loud it rocked her core. She'd always focused on her career, vowing it came first. "A handsome guy like you... I would think women would be falling at your feet all the time."

All of a sudden jealousy surged at her own words. Shocked at her reaction, she tapped them down.

Nor was she the only one surprised.

Madden choked as if hot chocolate went down the wrong pipe. When he stopped coughing, he swept errant hair behind an ear, but it flopped forward almost immediately. "Not anyone I'm interested in. I had a girlfriend, but we went our separate ways. Being a farmer's wife didn't appeal to her. I want an equal, someone to love, to be my best friend."

With those words Cobie knew she could care for this decent man. He was a rare specimen and those kinds of men came along once in a life time. She remembered those women from college and the ones she'd met after graduation who fell in love, married, had kids and gave up their careers. At the time, she'd thought them hare-brained.

Now…she understood.

She freed a soft sigh. If only she had met Madden under different circumstances. After she'd built a reputation in her vocation. They could have built a future together. Nothing could come with starting a relationship.

Gazing into his eyes, she made up her mind. "What if I said, I want to help you."

"With what…finding the right woman? Or are you offering to loan me a huge infusion of cash?"

"Sorry, no cash."

"Oh." The corners of his mouth lifted. "You have a candidate in mind for a wife, then?"

Like a fool, something deep and primal urged her to raise her hand and volunteer to be that woman. Slow down, girl. Take a deep breath. Another alternative had to exist, instead of becoming his wife. Though that wasn't a bad idea.

She wasn't going anywhere…not with the roads closed. She might as well put the time to good use and pay back his hospitality. Made sense to her. At least that was the logic she used to convince herself.

"Just hear me out."

Madden rose and lowered himself to the chair opposite her, a doubtful look on his face. "As long as you're not trying to convince me to sell."

"I want to help you…" She missed his closeness on the sofa and tried to focus on topic. "My expertise is in marketing and advertising and branding. Land acquisition for Stapler Construction is new for me. When their established clients want an update, I rebrand their look while the company refurbishes their buildings." Doubt flashed across Madden's face in the form of raised eyebrows. She had to talk fast, convince him of her legitimacy or she'd lose him. "You heard of Belfair Mall south of here. Remember when it got a whole new look a couple years ago. I was assigned the task of creating a new image for the mall in the consumer's mind. During construction, I had to make people see the mall as the ultimate location. It's called branding. That was my project, and I'm proud to say it was a success."

His eyes widened with awareness. "One of my mom's favorite places to shop. I remember some of the stores stayed open during construction."

She nodded, glad she didn't have to expend too much energy explaining. "Tell me how you make money from the farm. Just a broad overview. The basics."

That doubtful expression returned in a flash. "Why?"

"Because I need to know what you're doing if we're going to turn the business around. Tell me how you run this place."

Madden's storm grey gaze reflected the blue in the living room as if taking it in for the first time. He settled on the tulip pillow she hugged to her chest. "We sell tulips, along with a few other bulbs. Mostly during the festival. There's a two-month window when the crowds come. The retail store is open all year-round. We sell our left-over bulbs, knick-knacks, snacks, etc."

"And if this weather continues…what then?"

"It'll clear eventually."

She appreciated his optimistic attitude. He wasn't a man to give up easily. A drop of Irish blood must run in his veins, she thought with a smile. "And what if the crowds don't appear."

His scowl from earlier morphed into a frown. He wasn't happy hearing bad news, then who did? "I've got loyal customers we ship bulbs to."

"What percentage of your business is that?"

"Not much. Maybe five-ten percent. Another twenty goes to local stores."

"I see. That's not enough revenue to survive, is it?"

"Not really. My profit margin is pretty slim. I'd have to lay off my employees, but that's not how I operate. Grampa said employees always come first if a business is to succeed. You take care of them and they'll take care of the business."

Like a puzzle, pieces began to fit together in her mind. "Do you have a website? An on-line presence?"

"Sure. We list all our bulbs on it."

The dog shifted next to her. She laid her hand on him and he settled down. "What about the cut flowers?"

"We sell a few bouquets in the store during the festival."

She needed to think. "What happens to those you don't sell?"

He fidgeted in his seat. "We discard them."

"Isn't that like throwing money away? Show me your website." She set the pillow aside.

Madden straightened, a gleam in his eyes. "I'll get my laptop."

Cobie leaned her head back on the sofa. Ideas whirled. For her plan to work, Madden would have to change his *modus operandi*. Was he the type of man to change?

He returned to the living room with a laptop. He set it on the coffee table, flipped open the lid, and logged on. A couple seconds later he swiveled the screen toward her.

"Here it is."

She studied the image for a moment. Bright, clear pictures of blooming tulips filled the screen. Colorful rows of flowers went on forever. She clicked the next page. Individual pictures of bulbs with descriptions and prices were listed beneath each one. Next she checked the 'About Us' link, which gave a brief history of the farm, directions, and store hours.

"Pretty good website," he said when she didn't comment.

"It can use an update. When was this created?"

"Maybe twenty years ago. The only thing we've done recently is to add dad's creations when they were ready. No need to change something that works just fine."

She knew he was serious, so only nodded. "Websites should be tweaked annually."

He pressed back into the cushions of the chair, a huge smile on his face. "What have you got in mind?"

"I'm working on it."

CHAPTER EIGHT

"Work faster?" Madden said in a voice laced with light-hearted teasing.

Cobie looked twice at the handsome man and laughed, glad he wasn't shutting her down, that he appeared open to her proposal. In fact, she would say he acted much more receptive this time around.

"Yes, sir," she said, letting her voice chime with amusement.

"Want to give me a clue?"

Questions were always good. The right ones implied a willingness to become engaged in the conversation. "This storm is going to put a burden on a lot of people. Icy roads are going to prohibit them from getting out and about. Well, except for big-rig truck drivers, mail carriers, pizza delivery..." She stopped to dredge up additional occupations that would continue to work in the inclement weather.

In the lull, Madden spoke, "Utility workers. There's bound to be power outages. Plow truck drivers. Those who deliver groceries."

She warmed to the idea of working with him, and it helped that he came up with suggestions. They functioned well together. "I have some experience with websites. We'll start with that. Would you let me tweak yours? I could do it right here."

"Go for it. Especially if it keeps you off your leg." He gave her a serious look.

She froze, and anxiety shot through her. "What?"

"I was just thinking you might be comfortable in different clothes. Laura left some sweats, in case she comes over and needs to work in the fields. If you'd like, you can take a shower and change into them. You're more than welcome to do so."

A deep warmth spiraled through her as the initial sense of alarm subsided. "Thanks. Maybe I'll take you up on the offer."

"Great. I'll be in the basement for a while. I still need to finish a few things down there."

Cobie scooted to the edge of the sofa. Her heart twisted. She didn't want him to leave. She'd grown accustomed to him being close, but understood the dedication.

"See ya." Madden stood, took a step, then stopped. "I'll put a stool in the tub for you. That way you won't have to stand to shower."

His kindness deserved a response. "After I'm done, I'd be glad to lend you a hand before I start my project."

"That's okay. I'd prefer you to clean up and stay off your ankle. You're welfare is important to me."

"I'm not an invalid."

"As long as you're with me, you're my responsibility. And I take care of those important to me."

Important. Cobie didn't believe he meant his words the way she interpreted them. *Not her*. She raised her leg into the air. "Look, the swelling is going down."

"Bruising never belongs on a pretty lady."

Cobie's cheeks heated at the compliment. "It's fading...that's because I have had a wonderful nurse tending to me. Suppose I should reward him. You think he'd like a bouquet of flowers?"

Those marvelous grey eyes turned a darker shade as they widened. "He'd probably prefer a kiss."

The instant the words left his mouth, Madden turned his head away. "Sorry, I shouldn't have said that."

Her hormones went into over-drive at the thought of kissing him. She refused to let his comment pass. "Sounds like a good idea to me."

An awkward silence separated them.

Madden's gaze swept the room before returning to her. "I better go."

A sinking sensation made Cobie to fight to breath. Mortification followed on its heels. She'd made a fool of herself, answering in that manner. Maybe she was imagining her feelings and Madden didn't share the same sentiments as her. "Guess I'll take that shower you suggested."

He nodded. "After I'm done downstairs, I'll fix us a light lunch. Any requests?"

With shame still burning the tips of her ears, she brushed off his kindheartedness. "Just surprise me."

Watching him leave, her heart followed. She'd never fallen for a man so hard, so quickly. Then again, she'd never met one like Madden.

His steps faded as he went downstairs. A sigh fell out of her lips as she set the laptop on the coffee table. Grabbing the crutches, she put weight on her uninjured foot and powered herself to a wobbly stand.

In the bedroom, she found a set of grey sweats that would fit. She tossed the clothes over her shoulder and made her way into the guest bathroom.

Life was throwing a handsome obstacle in her path and she liked the potential it brought.

****

Madden's chest had swelled with the idea of kissing Cobie. She was a temptation hard to resist and he swore she would be worth kissing. She wasn't like Carolyn at all. There wasn't a spoiled bone in her body, and he genuinely enjoyed spending time with Cobie. He felt a connection to her, as if they'd known each other all their lives.

What harm would one kiss cause?

Whoa.... Everything was moving fast. Too fast.

While desire sky-rocketed, he told himself to slow down. He'd only known her for a day. Oh, love at first sight existed. His parents were proof of that. They'd met on a blind date and knew they were right for each other from the very start.

Maybe this was simple hormones. Infatuation or lust. Cobie Brooks deserved better from him. She was beautiful, thoughtful. He suspected she didn't appreciate being dependent upon anyone, and deserved respect.

And one other thing... Cobie's body contained soft curves in all the right places that he ached to caress.

The rattle of pipes and rushing water informed him she took a shower. His body responded to the image of water sluicing over her breasts, nipples wet, water curving over her waist and running down long legs. What he wouldn't give to join her. He'd suds her back, breasts, and between her legs. He swallowed hard at the image his mind created.

Shaking his head to expunge the fantasy, he checked the flower buds ready to bloom for the first time. Years of work would be visible very soon. He hoped Cobie could see them before she had to leave. He'd like to show her the results.

Suppressing his impatience, he finished the last set of seeds, put labels with the year and bulbs on the bin, brushed off his hands and rushed up the stairs. The view out the window of wintery weather prompted him to open a can of tomato soup and begin fixing toasted cheese sandwiches. Nothing like comfort food on a cold day.

He filled Gizmo's food dish and added ice cubes to his water bowl. The dog always drank water with cubes in it. Nothing like a spoiled dog.

Humming while working, he flipped over golden-brown sandwiches just as Cobie appeared in a pair of dark grey sweats, her blonde hair combed straight back and her sweet, heart-shaped face make-up free. Simply beautiful.

"Hi, there," he said, smiling. "Take a seat. Food will be ready in a jiff."

"You really are spoiling me," Cobie responded, face pinkened from hot water to a shade that added just the right color to her cheeks.

"You're worth it," he said, meaning it.

Half-way through eating, the faint thud of a car door almost didn't seem real. Madden glanced out a window but no vehicle appeared in the driveway and he couldn't see the retail store's parking lot from the kitchen window. Who would be there in this weather? Not Todd. He would have called before heading over. Susan and the other employees too. He dismissed the sound as his imagination.

He cleaned up the dishes after they ate and they went to sit in the living room.

"Here's my idea for keeping your doors open… We're going to convince people they need to buy tulips for those who gave them a helping hand during this storm. It'll be a way to say thank you to anyone— neighbors who checked on neighbors, delivery people, truck drivers."

"Come again," he said when she paused.

"We hit the internet with advertising. It doesn't cost a lot to make an ad, especially if I create it with the pictures you have on your website. You can give me your client list and I'll create an email that we can blast them with. Marketing is all about creating, communicating, and delivering a product that customers want. We're going to convince shut-ins that they need to show their appreciation by sending flowers. Everyone loves flowers, especially tulips."

He leaned over and covered her hands with his. "Great idea, but the flowers in the fields haven't formed buds yet."

"Doesn't matter," she answered, taking a deep breath. "Think of them as books. Books are put up for pre-sale all the time. Why can't we do the same with the tulips?"

Her voice tickled him. Cobie was right about love and he'd be standing at the head of the line for some, especially if it included her in the picture. He shoved aside his own insecurities, determined to let her know his feelings. The maelstrom of emotions were real and he had never shirked his duties in his life. Their relationship sat on a precipice and he wanted to see it blossom into something beautiful.

"I think you're right," he said, leaning forward to kiss her. Her lips softened as his touched hers and he started to draw her closer.

A loud knock interrupt them and they broke apart to stare at the front door.

Madden's strides ate up the distance between the sofa and the door. He'd get rid of whoever it was and return to kissing Cobie. He opened it to find a tall man with midnight dark hair sticking out from under a cap.

"Is Cobie Brooks here?" he said, frowning.

Shock rippled down Madden's spine. "Who are you?"

"Ronnie LeClaire. My sister sent me to bring Cobie home. With her stupid little car, she won't be able to drive for days."

"Ronnie, you didn't have to drive here to get me," Cobie said from the sofa. "Mr. Westerdahl has been kind enough to offer me his hospitality."

The man stepped around Madden without requesting permission to enter. "Yvonne was worried about you. Me too."

Madden pulled his brows together as he swiped his hair back. He wasn't sure what he was hearing, but didn't like the possessive tone of the newcomer. "What do you want to do, Cobie? You're more than welcome to stay until you can drive your own car. Your call."

Blinking, her blue eyes widened like a deer caught in headlights, she sat frozen on the sofa with the computer in her lap.

He held his breath, while she held his heart in her answer.

CHAPTER NINE

Sitting on the sofa, Cobie stared at the two men—equally tall and each with just the right muscular mass—one with thick blond hair that never stayed in place and grey eyes that flashed silver or reflected elements of different colors within them, the other with indigo-black hair and blue eyes the color of a summer sky.

Ronnie had hinted, rather strongly, of developing a relationship. She'd always been polite, due to her friendship with his sister, but never returned his interest because of his domineering attitude. Once, she'd even tried to explain her feelings to Yvonne, but evidently the message hadn't been passed along to him.

At the moment Ronnie's brows pinched together in a clear sign of anger, as if she'd done something wrong and he had the right to disapprove of her actions. Well, he was wrong. Big time.

Flicking her gaze to Madden, the worry glistening in his eyes grabbed her heart. She'd barely known him longer than twenty-four hours. Falling head-over-heels in love seemed so far-fetched to her. She couldn't believe it was happening to her...but it was...had.

Looking away, her gaze settled on the ebony-haired man, still shocked at his unexpected appearance. "You didn't have come all this way for me. Madden has been an excellent host while I've been stranded."

Her words wiped the smugness off Ronnie's face. He took another step closer. "I would have come sooner, but Yvonne just told me this afternoon you were stuck in Mt. Vernon. She gave me her cell so I could find you. You should have gotten rid of your car the last time it snowed. Piece of junk."

"I love BB and have no intention of selling her."

He eyed the empty plates and bowls on the coffee table where she and Madden had shared a tasty and cozy lunch. "I've come to take you home. You should be at your own place, among friends."

His overbearing attitude rubbed her wrong until Cobie's stomach tightened. She didn't need this... Not now. Not in front of Madden. "Maybe I like it here."

Out of the corner of her eye, she saw Madden rise. He stepped over to the sofa and stood behind her. His closeness was both calming and protective. She liked the sensations.

"Well, I don't like you being with a stranger." Ronnie gave her a sweeping glance. "And what the heck are you wearing? Get your things."

Her Irish temper rose. Cobie swore under her breath, at her wits end. "Excuse me?"

"You heard me."

"And you heard me."

Madden squeezed her shoulder. The comforting touch was all she needed. Time to diffuse the situation and set Ronnie LeClaire straight. And quickly.

"What's the matter with you? You're my girlfriend." The black-haired man wasn't backing down.

She gasped at the absurdity. "Wrong. You're not my boyfriend. Nor do you have any jurisdiction over me."

"We dated!"

"No, we did not. We had drinks with your sister a couple times. That's all."

"I planned to change that."

A low growl wrapped around her. She couldn't tell if the sound came from Gizmo or Madden. She rested her hand on the dog and his tense body relaxed. Patting his head seemed to reassure him.

"By bullying me into it? No thanks."

"This is for your own good. I'm taking you home." No contrite expression or apology in the man's tone or expression. One long step brought him to the edge of the coffee table.

"Stay."

This time there was no mistaking the soft word fell from Madden's mouth. His presence behind her melted her insides.

Ronnie's thin nostrils flared as he glared blue daggers at Madden. "She's coming with me."

"No, I don't think so. I'm not leaving my car indefinitely."

"The damn car will be fine in the parking lot." Ronnie glanced at Madden. "You don't mind, do you?"

"As a matter of—"

"Thanks, man," Ronnie interrupted. "I'll drive up as soon as the side roads are clear. That thing is worthless in snow or ice."

Cobie stiffened in her seat, her anger growing. "I might have something to say about you making decisions for me. I think you'd better leave."

Ronnie leveled a hard gaze at her. "I know what's best for you. Yvonne told me she warned you it was going to snow, but you didn't listen. Look what happened?"

"Yes, look what happened," she snapped back, thinking of her budding attraction to Madden. She had no idea where it would lead to, but wanted to find out.

Ronnie paused at her tone, his fists tightening. A flash of confusion knotted his brows, and for the first time he seemed to notice her foot propped on the tulip pillows.

"What's wrong with your foot? How'd you get hurt?"

"I slipped in the parking lot. Twisted my ankle. The swelling has gone down since I've kept it elevated. Madden has been kind enough to tend to my needs."

"That just proves you should be home." Arrogance laced Ronnie's voice.

"I'm sorry you don't care for the choice I've made." She gritted her teeth. "If Madden doesn't object, I'm staying until I can drive BB home."

Madden's warm touch brought comfort and relief...and something she couldn't put her finger on. "No objection from me."

Her heart pounded at the soft words coming from him. It dawned on her that thoughts of him jammed her mind. Half the time she forgot about the pain in her ankle. When it came to him, she wanted to be more than a friend. "Thank you."

"All my pleasure." Madden's hand on her shoulder tightened ever so slightly. She doubted he even knew, but she felt the subtle change. "You heard the lady. She's staying," he said to Ronnie.

Fury leapt out of the Ronnie's eyes; his lips thinned. Clearly, rejection wasn't on his agenda. He stepped toward her, his hand reaching for her.

In the blink of an eye, Madden blocked Ronnie's path. "Cobie's given you her answer. Now, get out of my house."

Ronnie's expression twisted into an ugly sneer and blue ice shot from her to Madden, then back to her. "You're making a big mistake, Cobie."

She inhaled, more determined than ever. Raising her chin, she glared at the tall man. "Then it's my mistake to make. Good bye, Ronnie. Tell Yvonne I'll call her soon."

The black-haired man spun on his heels and marched out the door.

Gizmo cracked one loud bark as if to say 'good riddance' and thumped his tail on the sofa next to her. Evidentially her resolve met with the dog's approval. She rubbed his ears.

Madden returned from shutting the door, flipping the lock, and sank into the chair.

"I'm sorry about that," she tried to apologize.

"You've got nothing to be sorry about."

Cobie held her breath and tried to relax. If she had been alone, Ronnie would have badgered her until she gave in. If that didn't work, she suspected he would have physically tried to force her to leave with him.

The two men weren't anything alike. Madden would never bully a woman into doing something against her will. It didn't take a genius to know he was a man worth giving up a career for.

The thought shocked her. It was a step she never anticipated taking for many years. Would anything come of it? Only time would tell.

****

Madden's chest expanded. He inhaled deep breaths to calm his rapid heartbeat. Moments ago adrenaline had coursed through his veins while the other man had demanded Cobie leave. Only sheer willpower had kept him from leaping over the sofa and beating the guy to a bloody pulp.

Now, he couldn't believe Cobie stayed. His feet walked on air.

Of course, the LeClaire guy had been a jerk. He'd seen his kind before…in college, in the service. They used their size to intimidate smaller people and get their way. He made the decision years ago it wasn't going to happen to anyone while he was around, especially to someone special like Cobie.

Leaning back in his chair, he tried to pretend everything returned to normal. Oh, hell! Nothing would be normal again. And he couldn't be happier.

"Who was that guy?" he asked.

Cobie pursed her lips for a moment. "Someone who made the wrong assumption. Ronnie has a tendency to be bossy. His sister, Yvonne, and I are co-workers. She wanted me to hook-up with him. I told her it wasn't going to happen. I guess she didn't take no for an answer."

"Don't think he did either," Madden said in a low voice. "For a moment there, I thought the situation was going to break bad. Though if reversed, I can't blame him. You're worth fighting for." He paused, his emotions screaming that this woman filled his heart and mind with lustful thoughts that he wanted to explore, but he feared to push too hard, too fast. "Maybe I'm being presumptuous…" She aimed those striking blue eyes in his direction and he knew he was lost. "I think you rock those sweats. You look gorgeous."

Genuine laughter spilled out of her. "Thanks. I needed that."

He transferred from the chair to the sofa, and nudged Gizmo aside. Not an easy task moving a seventy-five-pound dog. Luckily, he didn't object. Madden deliberately kept his hands to himself, even though his fingers itched to cradle her in his arms. "I know this is happening fast, but I gotta say it. I'm falling in love with you."

She touched his arm. "I think I am in love with you, too."

His pulse jumped. He heard a bit of hesitancy yet took her answer as a positive one and swept her in his arms, smelling the trace of shower remaining on her skin. The scent of soap and woman appealed to him on a gut level, igniting hormones inside him. He wanted to wake up in the morning with her next to him, roll over, and kiss her before starting his day.

"It's hard to describe my feelings when I'm with you. I'm happy. Little troubles seem to fade away. I want you in my life to share all the things that make living worthwhile. Having you around makes the world a better place. I might be jumping to conclusions, but I can hardly wait for my parents to return so I can introduce you to them. They're going to love you."

"Love must be contagious because I agree with everything you've said. I feel like I'm on a rollercoaster—it's terrifying, exhilarating—and I wouldn't want to experience this with anyone else."

Eyeing Cobie and enjoying the vision, he grinned. "Want to play cribbage? I'll give you a chance to beat me."

"Oh, you're on," she said with a laugh that melted his heart.

They spent the next couple hours playing cards and asking each other questions about themselves. To Madden, their bond strengthened.

"Afraid this is the last round," he announced. "I've got to finish downstairs. No rest for the wicked."

A twinkle materialized in Cobie's eyes. "Wicked? You? You've been the perfect gentleman."

"I can get wicked. Give me a chance and I'll be happy to show you." He stood and winked. "I won't be long."

"Can I help?"

"Having you here is all I need." He kissed the tip of her nose and left.

Working with the tulips had always been his passion. Now, going down the steps, he practically skipped, knowing the woman upstairs meant the world to him. He flicked on the light to check the flowers he'd created his last year of high school. This was the first-year flower buds had formed and he expected them to reveal their new species any day.

Under the bright glow of LED lights, a solitary bud had opened and bloomed in all its glory. The sight stopped him in his tracks. His next thought was he had to show Cobie, share it with her, but the bin was too full to carry upstairs.

"Cobie!" he yelled. "You gotta see this."

CHAPTER TEN

Madden heard the distinctive sound of crutches thumping across the floor overhead through the living room, heading toward the basement door and his heart stopped. God, maybe he shouldn't have shouted... What if Cobie fell? If she hurt herself, it would be his fault.

"Stop! I'll be up with the surprise," he hollered again.

The clomping stopped.

"Everything okay?" Cobie asked from the open doorway above.

Relief flooded him. He squeezed his eyes shut and managed to slow his heartrate to normal. "You're not going to believe this. Stay there. I'll come up."

****

Cobie's heart went straight to her throat and froze. At Madden's first shout, the inflection in his voice had held an edge that frightened her. For a split second she'd feared he'd hurt himself, that he needed help.

"What is it?" she asked from the top of the stairs, curiosity taking over.

His footsteps thundered on the staircase. "My high school project has bloomed. Look."

He pressed a solitary tulip into her hand. She studied the bell-shaped flower, then lifted her gaze to stare into a sea of happiness in his grey eyes. "It's blue."

He wrapped his arms her waist. Crutches tumbled to the floor and he swept her off her feet to swing her around in a circle. Gizmo jumped to avoid the falling crutches and stared at them as if they'd lost their minds.

And maybe they had.

"A true blue. I'm going to call it Cobie's Eyes, after you."

Her eyes widened. "I thought Westerdahls named their flowers after family members."

"We do."

Confusion niggled at the back of her head. Maybe she misheard him. The pressure of being held in Madden's arms seemed to increase slightly. She couldn't help herself and leaned into the hard warmth of his body when his hold lessened.

Perplexed, afraid to ask for clarification, she murmured, "Oh. It's beautiful, but how awful. Why'd you cut the poor little flower? Doesn't the bulb need the flower to gather energy so it can bloom again?"

A low chuckle slipped from Madden. "It's okay. There were plenty of others to replace it. I wanted to share the very first one with you." His chin settled on the top of her head, then he lifted her chin with his index finger. "Guess I should make this official. I'd like you to be part of the family… That is, if you'll marry me."

A shudder of delight rippled through her. This must be what being head-over-heels in love felt like. It had only been forty-eight hours since they first met. It seemed too good to be true.

While the words were her heart's desire, her practical nature shouted that it was only fair to offer him an out. "Are you sure excitement hasn't warped your viewpoint? We barely know each other. This is being rash and I never took you for a rash man."

"You're the right woman for me. And, I hope I'm the right man for you, Cobie Brooks. We'll have the rest of our lives to learn about each other."

"Madden…"

He kissed her, hard, fast.

That settled it. She made her choice on the spot. Wrapping her arms around his neck, she returned his kiss with her heart and soul.

When he raised his head to stare into her eyes, her heart knew she drew the right conclusion.

"I love you," he said. "I'll take that for a yes."

He left the crutches on the floor and carried her to the sofa. Gizmo must have sensed the joy and excitement, because his tail wagged a mile a minute. When the dog jumped up and started to lay next to Cobie, Madden blocked him.

"Not this time, buddy. That's my spot from here on out."

The dog moved away and took up residence at the far end of the sofa.

Cobie laughed, thrilled at the turn of events, and realized she still held the blue tulip. "I think you upset him."

Madden volunteered one of those grins that altered his face into something special. "Too bad, he's going to have to get used to me not sharing you."

"Since we left my crutches in the hall, can I talk you into putting this in a vase? I'd like to keep it for as long as possible." She held out the tulip.

"Sure thing." He jumped to his feet, a twinkle gleaming like silver in his grey eyes.

In a matter of minutes, he returned with a bud vase. He took the flower and set it in the vase, then put the pair on the coffee table where they both could admire it.

As he sat down, he draped an arm over her shoulder. "Did you know it was raining? Hard."

"I was just getting ready to let you know when you called me."

He tugged her closer. "It looks like the snow will be gone tomorrow."

"It's the weekend. I'm not in any hurry to go anywhere."

****

Monday morning, between breaks in the inclement weather, Cobie and Madden wore raincoats and rubber boots to stand between the rows of tulips piercing through the last of the snow. A pineapple express had swept in from the Pacific Ocean and the temperature rose to melt all evidence of the storm. The ground thawed. Puddles formed. Green stems thrived in the fields, some with tiny bud heads forming. In the far distance, mountain peaks ringed the valley.

Gizmo trotted down one of the numerous aisles, clearly pleased to be outside and stretching his legs.

Cobie inhaled a deep breath and smelled spring in the air. She felt like the luckiest woman in the world. She refused to question her choice. No second thoughts.

Hand-in-hand, they walked down the rows. She had called in sick at work, unwilling to leave Madden. When they stopped in the middle of the field, she leaned against his wide chest, the faint beat of his heart comforting to hear.

Madden's arms tightened over her. "I've always considered tulips the most beautiful flower in the garden—the jewel in the garden—but now I see something far more beautiful. You are the real jewel in my garden."

Warmth spiraled through her body at his words. "You make me feel beautiful. Special."

"It's no effort at all. You never have to leave, you know. Move in with me."

Her world tilted with the realization that she wasn't exactly in a hurry to head back. A thousand details rushed through her head. How was she going to move her stuff? Close her apartment? Those questions were for another time, she decided.

Only one mattered. "I do have a job."

Madden released his hold to capture her fingers. He pressed them to his chest, his grey eyes full of warmth. "I wouldn't dare think of suggesting you quit. Just the idea of knowing you'll return at the end of day is all I need to make me happy."

She never imagined she could have both family and career. It seemed like a dream come true. "Really?" Giggling, she contained the urge to do a one-legged happy dance.

Kissing her fingers, Madden released her hand to wrap his arms across her front and rocked her from side-to-side. "I've got the next fifty/sixty years with you in my life. I'm going to treasure every one."

His deep voice thrummed in his chest and Cobie leaned closer. She took a deep breath, catching the trace of his aftershave mixed with the fresh air. "Life is certainly going to be interesting with you."

For several seconds neither spoke. Instead, they watched Gizmo chase invisible objects.

Madden broke the silence by clearing his throat. "Let's hope so. A happy-ever-after life with you is all I want."

A WORD ABOUT THE AUTHOR...

Award-winning author Darcy Carson grew up reading everything her mother brought home from the library. Reading romances became her favorite topic. Eventually her love of those novels led her to start writing them. She resides in a Seattle suburb with her husband and a prince of a poodle.

Other books by the author

Self-Published Anthologies:

Spring Reads

Christmas Reads

Beach Reads

The Wild Rose Press: Dragons Return Series:

She Wakes the Night

Woman in the Woods

He Walks in Dreams

Self-Published: Magic Police Series:

Magic in the Air

Long Distance Romance

Pam Binder

Coincidence is just another word for magic.

CHAPTER ONE

Melody McBride stuffed long-stemmed yellow roses into the garbage disposal in the kitchen of the Matchmaker Café on Lake Union. The morning was the perfect Seattle day in May. It had rained briefly last night and this morning the sun shone in the blue-bird clear sky, making the city sparkle like a new penny.

Inside the café with its round tables, the walls were decorated with framed scenes of the Irish countryside, white-washed stoned cottages, and photos of brightly painted Irish doors in reds, blues, yellows, and greens. The doors were reminiscent of the real doors, collected from all over the world and displayed on the walls of the matchmaker's flagship café in a suburb near Seattle. It was too early to welcome customers and for once, Melody wasn't enjoying the quiet. It gave her too much time to think.

She stuffed more roses into the disposal. They were an apology bouquet sent by her boyfriend, Prince William Campbell IV. Six months after a whirlwind Christmas romance, Melody's memories of the prince-that-stole-her-heart still stung. He hadn't technically "got away". It was more a case of the times they spent together were fewer and further apart, which sent the message that it was over. How could she have been such a fool?

Her long-distance relationship with the prince was on shaky ground. She had visited him on his estate in New Zealand a few times and he had made one trip to Seattle in February for Valentine's Day. That was the last time they'd been together.

Melody had met William when she and her aunts were planning a wedding on his yacht, with his father the intended groom. Then two months ago, her aunts had put her in charge of running the Matchmaker Café on Lake Union. Their hereditary matchmaking business was expanding. It had begun when her aunts came from Ireland a little under ten years ago and opened the first matchmaker café in Washington State. They'd expanded to the one on Lake Union and were looking at additional locations. As a result, Melody no longer had as much time to visit William as often as she would have liked. Then the phase where he would promise to visit, followed by a phone call canceling, and apology flowers, like the ones grinding in the disposal, began. If the disposal broke because of the flowers, and their fibrous stems, it would be one more sign that her relationship was over.

When they were together, William said how perfect they were for each other. He'd stopped short of asking her to marry him or suggesting she move to New Zealand. The constant cancelling of his visits wasn't helping her self-confidence.

Melody stuffed the last of the roses into the disposal. William had sent yellow roses, which to anyone else might have seemed perfect. But she was not only a matchmaker but a wedding planner and knew the meaning of a roses' color. A yellow rose was the symbol of friendship. She could give him the benefit of the doubt. How could he have known that yellow meant friendship? And perhaps she would have but she was freaking out. This was the third time in a row that he'd called to reschedule a visit. Third time's the charm, as the saying went. She didn't need a plane to fall from the sky to get the message. She suspected that the relationship, whatever it had been, was over.

She pressed her hand against her chest as her eyes welled with tears. She willed her heart to not care so much. His apologies always began with something like: "You know I'm run my family's business and my duties are important." Then ended with the classic: "But you are important to me as well and we will figure out how to make it work."

His words were beautifully spoken with the deep sexy New Zealand accent she'd grown to love.

She wanted to scream. Or cry. Whichever one made her feel better.

She flipped on the sink's disposal switch and watched the last rose disappear down the drain. The crunching sound reminded her of broken promises and shattered dreams. Her aunts thought she was overreacting. She believed she was being realistic. It was time to either confront him on where he saw their relationship headed or move on.

His idea of how-to-make-it work, was for her to drop everything and fly half-way around the world to visit him. In the last six months there had never been talk of marriage or of her moving to New Zealand to live with him. Both were big steps, and her life and family were in the Seattle area and she'd just taken charge of the Matchmaker Café on Lake Union. The bottom line, however, was that she didn't know how she would feel if asked. It felt as though her life was in limbo and if their relationship had a future.

This time his cancelation had not only accompanied apology-roses but two first-class tickets to New Zealand where his family owned an estate. He couldn't send the family jet, he explained, because his father had flown it to Europe. William had purchased two tickets as he said that the first-class side-by-side tickets would ease the grueling commercial airline flight that include two layovers. She told him she didn't need two tickets. As usual, he hadn't listened.

She reached for the tickets to stuff them down the disposal with the roses.

"I wouldn't do that if I were you," Aunt Casey said.

Her aunt entered the kitchen, wearing her signature green glitter eyeshadow to match her slacks and sweater. She was one of three aunts who had raised her after the death of Melody's parents. They were all eccentric and fun and the type of people who served brownies for breakfast.

This morning Aunt Casey had worn her salt and pepper grey hair piled on top of her head at an angle like the tower of Pisa. She yawned and put a kettle on the stove to boil water for her tea. "You should visit William in New Zealand."

Melody heaved a sigh. "Aunt Casey, we've talked about this. Visiting William will start out like all the others. The first twenty-four hours of my week-long visit will be great. He'll go on and on about all the places in New Zealand we'll visit. Then he will get called away for an emergency that will take anywhere from a few hours to a few days to sort out. The day my plane leaves to Seattle he will apologize and promise that the next time will be different. It never is. If only I knew where we stood. I plan to send him a message that it's over between us."

The whistle on the kettle sounded off as though in protest to Melody's comment. Aunt Casey turned the heat off on the stove, removed the kettle and poured water into her teapot over loose-leaf, Earl Gray tea. "If you really want to know where this relationship is headed, you have to ask William in person. Or be content that you could spend years dating without a clear-cut idea of where you stand." She set the kettle back on the stovetop. "There I've said my piece."

Melody knew her aunt was right. Her last boyfriend had broken up with her via text. Even though she had known that their relationship was over she had been devastated and had thrown her cell phone into Lake Union. A stupid move but proved how insensitive that method of communication had been for something as important as the status of a relationship. William deserved better. He was a good guy. It wasn't his fault he was a prince with a mountain of obligations since his father had turned running the family's business over to him.

She accepted the cup of steaming tea Aunt Casey offered and blew on it to cool it down. She stared at the loose tea leaves floating to the surface. Her aunt was on a loose-leaf kick, convinced the tea tasted better. Melody wasn't as convinced and there was always the issue of floating leaves that got stuck in her teeth. But her aunt did have a point.

"You win. I'll go."

"Remember to bring winter clothes and boots. It's autumn in New Zealand this time of year and can be cold and stormy."

Melody made a mental note to pack wool sweaters instead of sundresses. The eighteen-to-nineteen-hour time difference wasn't the only thing she had to contend with. Seattle and Newland's season were reversed. When springtime in Seattle, it was late fall in New Zealand.

She glanced outside the café. The sun had risen higher, and the rays of the spring sun danced over Lake Union like sequins on a party dress. Spring was her favorite time of the year. She'd waited all winter for the gloomy rain-soaked weather to disappear and flowers to bloom, and now that it had she was headed back into winter. The cold was just another thing she wasn't looking forward to experiencing. But she was backed against the wall. Cancelling her trip would only prolong the inevitable breakup.

Melody checked the time on her cell phone, gulped down her tea and set it on the counter. If she was to make the flight tonight, she needed to pack. "I won't need boots. I'll be staying at the estate and we never go anywhere."

She grimaced at how petulant she sounded, no matter that what she'd said was the truth. Just once, she'd like to behave like a tourist and take in the beauty of New Zealand. She longed to indulge in her inner geek and check out the locations of the movie sets. She'd heard some of her favorites, like *The Lord of the Rings*, *Avatar*, *The Chronicles of Narnia*, and *Game of Thrones* were filmed in New Zealand.

Casey retrieved Melody's cup, tilting it to one side and then the other as though reading the tea leaves. "Trust me. You're going to need boots."

CHAPTER TWO

Packing boots had been the least of Melody's worries. She'd changed outfits she planned to wear on the airplane five times, trying to figure out what image she'd like to portray when she met William at the Auckland airport. She discarded the black dress as too fancy, the long skirt and short sleeve blouse as impractical, and settled on comfortable slacks, a wool sweater, and her sneakers.

Her choice of wearing clothes she could jog through the airport in like a crazy person, had proven to be a wise choice.

Melody, one hand pulling her luggage, and the other gripping two tickets, raced for the departure gate for New Zealand at the Seattle airport. The airport was crowded, and the clatter of conversation drowned out rational thought. At least that was her excuse why she was late. She knew another one was that she was dragging her feet. She didn't want to get on the plane.

When her aunt had first dropped her off at the airport at six o'clock this evening for the nine o'clock flight Melody thought she had plenty of time to turn in one of the tickets William had sent. It felt ridiculous and indulgent to have two tickets.

The long lines seemed longer than normal, and it had taken an hour to find out that neither of the two first-class tickets William had sent could not be refunded back to his credit card and another hour to go through security and find her gate.

Out of breath, she rolled her suitcase up to the back of the line that indicated first class ticket holders just as it was announced that they were boarding.

On the bright side, her first-class seats reclined into a bed, so she'd have plenty of room to nap between flights. This last week she'd slept very little. She kept going over in her mind what she'd say to William when they were face-to-face. How did you end a relationship you wanted to keep?

A short distance away, a crash and a child's determined, "No, I won't go," broke through the airport's hum of activity.

Melody and a few others in line glanced over at the child who had disturbed their routine. The little girl was about five or six. Her long dark hair was braided down her back and she wore pink jeans and a wool cable knit sweater with tiny rose buds embroidered into the yarn. It looked like she had been the one who had pushed over the suitcase. She stood near the area reserved for passengers waiting to board in the coach section of the plane.

Despite her outburst, Melody smiled. The child was adorable, and Melody admired the child's ability to speak her mind. Melody envied the little girl. Melody had kept her unease about her stalled relationship with William to herself, instead of confronting him the last time they were together.

A tall man, with dark hair that looked tossed in the wind, and wearing a tan windbreaker and jeans knelt beside the little girl and although he talked to her in soothing tones. His voice, although low, still carried the short distance that separated him from Melody.

"Sweetheart," he said. "We have to board the plane. Don't you want to see Grandpa? He misses you."

The little girl's gaze slid toward the large window where the plane bound for New Zealand was visible on the tarmac. "Daddy, the plane is big and scary."

"You will have your very own seat on the plane," the father said reassuringly.

A tear rolled down the little girl's cheek. "Will they have Jaffas?"

"No, but I'll buy you the candy as soon as we land in Auckland."

The little girl sniffled and held up her arms for her father to pick her up and then buried her head on his shoulder.

Once the disturbance was concluded, the first-class line resumed moving forward as though the incident with the father and child had held it spellbound. People resumed their conversations, some complained of the long line, or misbehaving children, while others expressed their excitement of traveling to New Zealand. A flight attendant with a pleasant smile moved near the first-class line to smooth passenger's ruffled feathers and help the line move along faster.

Melody glanced at the father and child again. The child had fallen asleep in the father's arms. Traveling in coach, with two flight changes, would not be easy for them.

"Such a sad story," the flight attendant directing traffic said to Melody. "The father has been in Seattle with his daughter for the past three years while his wife underwent cancer treatment. She didn't make it and after trying to make a go of it in Seattle, he decided to return to New Zealand and help his cousin with the family business. Tragic. I tried to get he and his daughter upgraded but our plane is sold out. Oh look, it's almost your turn to check in."

Melody looked at the tickets she held. She knew exactly how it felt to lose a parent at a young age. Her aunts had tried to fill the void with love and Melody was grateful and loved them with equal measure. But the pain of loss never really went away. She glanced at her tickets again as her heart ached for the little girl and her father. She had to do something and then an idea took form.

Melody stepped out of line and addressed the flight attendant. "My boyfriend gave me two tickets and I'd like to give them to the father and his daughter in exchange for their tickets. Can you make that happen?"

CHAPTER THREE

Over twenty hours later Melody's plane landed in New Zealand. They were ahead of schedule. That was the good news. The bad news was that they hadn't landed in Auckland. The plane had been diverted to an alternate airport. Melody yawned as she finished going through New Zealand's customs and immigration.

She'd tried to nap on the plane but sleeping in an almost upright position hadn't worked. In addition, the minute she'd drifted off to sleep, it landed for the first of two layovers. She'd then had to gather her things, disembark, find a new gate, board the plane, and find her seat. Then as she drifted off to sleep again, the same thing happened all over again.

During each layover she'd looked for the father and little girl she'd given her tickets to but hadn't seen them. Perhaps their final destination hadn't been New

Zealand after all. On the final leg of her flight, she'd given up trying to sleep and watched reruns of *Game of Thrones*.

Then when it didn't seem that things could get any worse, the pilot's voice had boomed on the plane's intercom and informed the passengers that their flight from Seattle to Auckland had been diverted to the Wellington airport. Something about a storm and that passengers needed to make alternate plans when they landed. She almost welcomed the delay. She wasn't looking forward to confronting William, concerning their relationship.

But he deserved an update. William had planned to pick her up at the Auckland airport later this afternoon. She punched in William's number and got his leave-a-message beep. A small blessing. Whenever she heard his voice, her heart melted, and she remembered why she had fallen in love with him. She cleared her throat and ordered her heart and the little voice in her head that advised she wait a little longer to break up with him to back off. Waiting would only make things worse and more painful.

She cleared her throat as she spoke into the phone. "William? This is Melody. My plane landed earlier than expected but I'm not in Auckland. The plane was diverted to Wellington. I know you're busy, so no reason to fly down. It's early in the morning and I'll book another flight and be there this afternoon." She paused and added. "See you soon." She hung up the phone and stuffed it into her tote bag.

She had thought about saying, love you, as a closing, but decided against it. They'd never said the words to each other, which of course was at the heart of the issue. Besides, she reminded herself, she was breaking up with him.

Her heart thundered against her chest. The idea of breaking up hurt more than she had expected it might. She pushed down the feelings and jerked her suitcase toward the long lines at the ticket counters. Evidentially, she wasn't the only person in need of a new flight.

After waiting in line for what seemed an eternity, she approached the ticket counter and addressed the woman behind the computer. "Good morning. A one-way ticket to Auckland, please."

The woman behind the counter wore thick glasses, and a pinched expression and looked as frazzled as Melody felt. Dealing with unhappy passengers wasn't easy. The woman's smile looked forced. "We regret that all flights to Auckland are cancelled due to the weather conditions. No flights in our out until the storm passes."

"But I promised my boyfriend that I'd be in Auckland this afternoon." Melody shook her head, upset with herself that she'd been brisk with the woman. The weather and cancelled flights weren't the woman's fault. "Never mind. I apologize it's not your problem." She hesitated. "How far a drive is it from here to Auckland?"

"Five or six hours, depending on stops."

"Perfect. Where can I rent a car?"

"Downstairs and to your right. Next please."

Melody nodded a thank you and rolled her suitcase toward the direction the woman at the ticket counter had indicated, dialing William's number at the same time. His cell went to message yet again. She ground her teeth. Why did the man have a cellphone if he never bothered to answer his calls? What if this was a real emergency?

She took in a deep breath to calm down. She wasn't helpless. She could take care of herself. She recognized the signs of jetlag and blamed them on her frustration. She sucked in another breath. She needed to give William another update. At least one of them knew how to behave in an emergency.

"William," she said with an edge to her voice. "It's Melody again. I can't get a flight out today but I'm looking into renting a car. The ticket agent said the drive might take around six hours. I didn't sleep very well on the plane...long story. If I get too tired, I'll stop at a hotel along the way, which will make it a two-day journey. I'll call you with an update." She hesitated. "Call me if you get a chance." She ended the call and headed to stand in yet another long line.

The crowds had thinned out which Melody took as a good sign. The only issue was that there was only one counter open that advertised a car or taxi service. She knew it wasn't true, but she felt as though she'd spent as much time waiting in lines on this trip as she had flying in the air.

When it was her turn, she rolled up to the counter and pasted on a smile, remembering to be nice. It wasn't the man behind the counter's fault that she was in a bad mood. It felt like the world was conspiring to keep she and William apart.

She never should have listened to her Aunt Casey. Melody should have done what most people did these days. She should have broken up with William in a text. If she had any sense, she'd check into an airport hotel, and text William that it was over between them and then book the next available flight back to Seattle.

"May I help you?" The man wore a bowtie and the same dead-pan expression the woman at the ticket counter had had.

It occurred to Melody that the man and woman must have attended the same class on how to deal with disgruntled customers. "I'd like to rent a car, please. I need to drive to Auckland."

His deadpan expression held as his voice took on a mechanical tone. "I just rented the last auto. I'm very sorry. Check back in the morning."

The man flipped over the closed sign on the counter with a finality that set Melody's teeth chattering. Why did he ask if he could help her when he knew he didn't have any cars to rent? It was confirmed. The universe was conspiring against her and adding insult to injury, she was so tired she could barely stand let alone think rationally.

She hadn't slept more than a few hours in the last forty-eight. Outside the airport the wind howled like an angry beast and rattled the windows and her nerves at the same time. She glanced around the terminal. The few remaining passengers were either greeted by friends or family or headed outside. Everyone was in a good mood which only made her feel worse.

The man at the car rental counter had said to check back in the morning. That was a good idea. She shouldn't drive feeling as sleepy as she did. Maybe the universe was looking out for her after all. She needed sleep before she started her trek in a foreign country.

Vehicles in New Zealand, like England and Canada, were driven on the opposite side of the road from the U.S., and as yet she'd never driven a car in New Zealand. She'd only visited twice, but in each case, William had either driven, or a limo had taken them where they needed to go. William's house manager, Sedrick, a wonderfully kind man who reminded her of the actor, Anthony Hopkins, and liked to share stories of William as a child, had offered to teach her but she'd never taken him up on the offer.

She reasoned that she could figure it out, but not when she was this tired. Sleep would be the smart thing to do. In morning, with any luck, flights would have resumed, and she wouldn't have to deal with renting a car.

Melody yawned, looking over at a row of metal airport chairs lined up against the window. In her sleep deprived state, they looked comfy. Maybe she'd sleep at the airport. The chairs looked inviting and spending the night at the airport would assure that she was first in line in the morning to either rent a car or book the next available flight to Auckland…or Seattle.

She yawned again and yanked on her luggage, visualizing that she'd use one of the sweaters in her suitcase as a pillow.

Someone tugged on her coat. "Miss Lady?" The child's voice sounded familiar.

Melody looked down at the little girl with braids, recognizing her at once. It was the child she'd given her First-Class ticket to in Seattle. Before she could ask the child where her father was, he appeared, gently pulling the child from Melody's coat.

"I apologize for bothering you. We looked for you during the layovers but couldn't find you. Then just now my daughter mentioned that she saw you at the car rental counter. We wanted to thank you again for giving us your seats. That was very kind."

"You are welcome."

The child looked up at her father. "Daddy, ask her."

He smiled down at his daughter lovingly. "Thank you for reminding me sweetheart." He turned his smile on Melody. "Amelia overheard the man at the counter telling you that all his rental cars were booked and that you were headed to the Auckland area. We're headed in that direction as well and can give you a lift." He paused. "If you don't mind a detour to Matamata, that is. My daughter wants to see the Hobbit movie set."

"Actually, I'd love to see the movie set. But I couldn't impose."

His grin widened. "I assure you, I'm a good guy and the offer is sincere. If you need me to provide references, a background check, my latest credit score…"

There was no doubt in Melody's mind that he was a good guy. She and her aunts had an instinct about people and knew right away the person's true intentions. They liked to refer to this ability as one of their gifts. It was what they said made them such great matchmakers. Of course, it wasn't something easily explained, so they kept it to themselves.

She smiled. "Thank you, and there's no need for a background check. You, and your daughter are very generous. Yes, I'd love to hitch a ride with you." Melody held out her hand.

"We haven't met officially. I'm Melody."

The child grinned and, held out her hand. "My name is Amelia and my daddy's name is Oliver but everyone calls him Oly."

"I'm pleased to meet you both," Melody said, and meant every word. The day had just gotten brighter.

"I don't know about you," Oly said, "but Amelia and I are starving. As soon as we retrieve the rental car, would you like to get a Kiwi burger? I know a great restaurant close by the airport. Or are you one of those vegetarian types?"

She laughed. It felt good to laugh. It helped release the pent-up tension she'd been storing up for months. "I'm a red meat gal. Aren't Kiwi burgers the ones with a fried egg and beetroot?" When Oly nodded she continued. "I love them and couldn't get enough when I visited a short time ago. I tried to duplicate them in Seattle and failed miserably."

"The key ingredient is New Zealand's beef cattle."

Amelia tugged on Oly's shirt. "You promise we'd also buy Jaffas and Hokey Pokey Ice Cream."

Oly chuckled. "That I did. We'll have to wait until we get to Auckland. They have the best Hokey Pokey ice cream, but I'll make sure we have Jaffas for our ride to the Hobbit movie set."

"What are Jaffas?" Melody said.

"How is it that you've visited New Zealand but haven't heard about Jaffas?" Oly chuckled. "No worries. That is easily remedied. Come with us. You are in for a treat. Did you bring boots? It looks like it's raining mud outside."

CHAPTER FOUR

New Zealand's ocean coastline sped past Melody's passenger window as she settled back in her seat. Oly hadn't been joking when he said it was raining mud. But once they were underway on their road trip, the weather quieted and the clouds had thinned, allowing the sun to peek through. Everything seemed better on a full stomach and the promise of sunshine. Melody hadn't felt like eating on the plane and hadn't realized how hungry she was until she'd taken her first bite of the delicious Kiwi burger. The burger had lifted her spirits.

She and Oly hadn't said much since they'd turned onto the freeway. He seemed as locked in his thoughts as she was. Her issues with her stalled relationship with William, paled in comparison to

Oly's. He'd lost the woman he loved and faced the prospect of raising their daughter as a single parent.

Melody glanced over her shoulder toward the back seat. Amelia was sound asleep in her car seat, hugging a well-loved, chocolate brown stuffed teddy bear. "Your daughter is so sweet."

"Thank you. She is the light of my life." He paused as his grin widened. "Sometimes I think she's stronger than I am." He hesitated again, his eyebrows scrunching together. "I want to thank you again for exchanging seats with us. We had so much room and spent the time pretending we were flying on a giant silver dragon."

Melody laughed. "What a great idea. Was the dragon your idea or Amelia's?"

"Amelia's. She's like her mother. Great imagination and always looking on the sunny side. When it rained, even like earlier when it seemed like it was raining mud, Sarah would have had a way of spinning it into a positive. She'd say when it rained it was because the fairies were poking holes in the clouds. That always made Amelia smile. Me too."

"You miss her. "I'm so sorry."

Oly nodded, then blinked, swiping at his eyes. "Every day, especially when it rains for some reason. I guess its because I remember her stories." He cleared his throat. "The flight attendant told me that you had mentioned our situation, so you know that Amelia has had a lot of tragedy in her young life. That's why we've returned to New Zealand. I have good memories here and she needs to be with family." He glanced toward Melody. "So, you are traveling to New Zealand on your own, eh? There must be a story in there somewhere." He frowned. "That was rude. None of my business. Forget I asked."

Melody knew he was trying to change the subject. "I don't mind. There really isn't much to tell, though. I flew here to meet my boyfriend. We're trying to make the whole long distant relationship work." She glanced out the window. A breeze blew over the waves until they resembled ropes of frosting-shaped seashells on a wedding cake. The image took her by surprise, and she smiled to herself. "You mentioned that you grew up here," she said, wanting to keep the conversation going.

"Born and raised," he nodded with a smile and a soft chuckle. "Some say our family started settling here hundreds of years ago which potentially makes my ancestors pirates, criminals, crazy or a combination of all three. We're all boringly civilized now and own farms, cattle, and a bit of timberland up north."

"Cattle?" That explains why you said I couldn't duplicate the taste of Kiwi burgers in the States. I needed to use New Zealand cows."

"We are proud of our beef. The cattle ranch is where me and Amelia are headed. My family called and said they needed my help." A cloud moved over his expression. "The offer was made with love and the best of intentions. But if it hadn't been for Amelia, I may have refused. Families are complicated."

Melody smiled, thinking about her aunts and extended family. "I couldn't agree more. My family is not unlike yours in that I've heard rumors that we have had more than a few pirates and criminals occupying the family tree. We also have a family business that dates back hundreds of years as well. We're Irish matchmakers and event planners. It was during one of our events over last Christmas when I met my boyfriend."

"Christmas is a magical time to fall in love." His expression brightened as though kissed by a spring sun in the Pacific Northwest. "Meeting my wife, Sarah, wasn't as glamours as all that. I loved her the moment I first saw her. Her family had just moved into town and she was on the beach flying a red kite. I'd never seen a kite fly in the sky that high before. It looked like it could touch the clouds." He griped both hands on the wheel as his smile spread over his face. "She was in fifth grade and I was in sixth. It took me another five years before I got up enough courage to ask her out on a date. We married when we were still at university."

"That's a beautiful story."

"How about you? You said you met your fella when you were planning a wedding was it love at first sight?"

"Actually, I think it was." She hesitated. "I'm not sure where our relationship is going, however. That's the real reason I'm here. He's a really kind man and terribly busy with his work. I'm thinking he wants to end our relationship, but he is struggling to figured out a way to do it without sounding like a jerk."

"Do you still love him?"

"Unfortunately, yes. That's the problem. But I'm not going to be one of those people who holds on long after it's over. It wouldn't be fair to either of us. I'm one of those people who wants marriage and a family." She shook her head. "That sounds so old fashioned when I say it out loud."

"Old fashioned is a good thing. We need more of that in this world if you ask me. If you don't mind my asking, what is the bloke's name?"

Melody yawned again. "William Campbell. If you don't mind, I'm really tired. Jet lag is catching up with me. I think I'll take a nap."

"Sure. That wouldn't be Prince William Campbell IV, would it?"

She nodded and leaned her head against the window, closing her yes. "Yes. Do you know him?"

"A little."

****

A short time later, Oly glanced at his daughter in the rear-view mirror and then over toward Melody. Everyone was fast asleep. He eased off the main road onto a wide area where tourists stopped to take pictures of the rolling landscape. It was a little warmer, so he rolled down the windows, parked, got out of the car, and dialed his cousin's phone number.

It went straight to message.

"Hey cousin, Oly here. Amelia and I landed a few hours ago and are driving to Hobbiton first before heading to the estate. Now with that little piece of info out of the way I'll get to the real reason for the call. You'll never guess who is driving with me and Amelia to Auckland. The woman is a matchmaker named Melody. Funniest thing. She gave us her first-class tickets so we could fly in comfort while she was stuffed like a sausage in the back of the plane."

Oly glanced again in the car to make sure his companions were still sleeping, then pushed away from the car door and walked a few feet away. Each step made him more frustrated. He gritted his teeth, feeling his frustration grow. His cousin was an idiot for letting someone as nice as Melody slip away.

"Melody mentioned your name as the bloke she was coming to visit. I'm guessing that this is the woman you mentioned that you'd met in Seattle at Christmas time. The one you said you were in love with. You are a genius in business my friend but a colossal failure when it comes to relationships." Oly's voice rose. "You wanker. She doesn't think you love her. She's coming here to break up with you. Melody seems like a nice woman. The kind of woman who you build a future with, not someone you take for granted. How the hell did you screw this up? You have to make it right."

Oly ended the call and made one more then climbed into the car and headed back onto the road. The traffic was light, and they were making good time. He had made reservations for a private tour, but they still had to arrive before Hobbiton closed.

Melody stretched. "Did we stop? Are you sure you don't want me to drive?"

"I had to make a couple of phone calls and didn't want to wake you or Amelia. Thank you for the offer to drive, but I'm okay. Go back to sleep. In a short time, we'll stop at Lake Taupō for a short break. We may even have time to visit Huku Falls. I'll wake you when we arrive at Hobbiton."

She nodded a thank you and settled back against the passenger's window and drifted off to sleep again. Until today, he'd never interfered or made comments to

William regarding the women he dated. But Melody seemed different. Special. Oly only hoped his cousin realized it as well before it was too late.

CHAPTER FIVE

Miles away, William Campbell VI unloaded the large section of driftwood he'd planned to fashion into a table from his truck and set it on the back porch of his manor. He'd spent the better part of yesterday and today searching the coastline that bordered his family's estate for something this unique. The sea gave up its best driftwood treasures during the storm season.

He had solved a major crisis earlier than expected and knew he had time before Melody's plane arrived to search the beaches. He loved this time of year when he had less obligations. The farm, cattle and timberlands still had to be maintained and livestock fed but the days were shorter, and the cold weather gave him an excuse to spend more time inside. With any luck, and Oly's help, he would have more time to spend with Melody.

In past years he looked forward to this downtime where he could work on his hobby of turning driftwood into furniture. This year he had another reason. This year he planned to spend more time with Melody. She'd been on his mind a lot lately. He'd cancelled more trips to see her than he cared to admit but it couldn't be helped. The estate didn't run itself and he was sure Melody understood.

He liked their relationship the way it was. They saw each other when their schedules allowed. She was busy helping run her family's matchmaking business and he was busy with his. Neither of them had time for a long-term commitment. Things were good, and the best part was that he would see Melody this afternoon. He had time to shower and change before picking her up at the airport in Auckland.

With a spring in his step, he walked toward the house that a century ago had been built to resemble an English manor. He entered through the mud room and removed his boots and jacket. Sedrick, the long-time family's house manager, entered, wearing a dark suit, and holding out a towel in one hand and William's cell phone in the other.

Sedrick had been with the Campbell family since before William was born and was a trusted friend. Sedrick weathered face always reminded William of driftwood. It was unique and full of stories to tell.

"You have messages, sir."

The fact that Sedrick hadn't first asked William about his day was telling. "I presume you've listened to them already?"

"Of course, sir."

William didn't mind that Sedrick had listened to his messages. It had been William's idea. William often left his phone at the manor because the cell service in the remote areas of the estate were unreliable. "Was there anything important?"

Sedrick pushed his glasses up the ridge of his nose. "It is best you listen to them yourself. I did send someone out to find you."

William ignored the towel and took the phone, hearing the urgency in Sedrick's voice. "I drove farther down the coast than usual and camped overnight. The messages are important, then?"

"Quite. I've made tea and biscuits and brought them to the drawing room, although you might need a stiff drink."

William didn't like the seriousness in Sedrick's tone. Something was wrong. William punched in his security code. He followed Sedrick to the drawing room where a fire blazed in the hearth as he listened to his messages. The first few were routine business questions that could wait to be answered in the morning. There was also one from his father announcing that he and his wife had extended their visit in France. So far there was nothing that warranted Sedrick's worried expression.

He listened to Melody's first message and his heart sank. "Melody already arrived. She's in Wellington. I need to leave. Damn. Father has the jet."

"Keep listening, sir. You should sit down. I'll pour you a cup of tea. There is also a message from your cousin, Oly."

There was something in Sedrick's manner that worried William. He sat in the chair near the stone fireplace as Sedrick served tea. When Sedrick moved to stand a short distance away, William listened to Melody's first message again then listened to the others. He repeated the process a second time, praying that he hadn't heard the pain in Melody's voice and the warning in Oly's.

"Melody's plane was diverted to Wellington and she's driving here with Oly," William said as though to himself. "The last message was from Oly. Somehow my cousin, Amelia and Melody connected and he's driving Melody here after they visit Hobbiton."

"Miss Amelia always did like the Hobbits," Sedrick said in a flat tone. "I'm glad the producers kept the movie set. It's quite the tourist attraction. Didn't Amelia ask you and her father to build her a Hobbit house on the estate before her mum got sick?"

William nodded absently, fully aware that Sedrick had sidestepped the real issue. Melody wanted to break up with him and Oly thought he was an idiot. They had been more like best friends than cousins, and William trusted Oly's opinion. Oly was a good man. William had been heartbroken for him when he learned of Oly's wife's death two years ago. William had extended him an open invitation to return and help him run the estate whenever he was ready and was overjoyed when his cousin had taken William up on the offer a few weeks ago. Families were important.

William sat forward in his chair, processing Oly and Melody's messages as he tried to figure out what to do next. He kept to a safe subject as he tried to process the messages. "I finished the Hobbit house while Oly and Amelia were living in Seattle. I wanted it to be a surprise when they returned. I'd hoped it might cheer Amelia after her mum's…" William combed his hands through his hair and set his cell on a table beside his chair. "Melody wants to end our relationship," he said, no longer being able to contain his disbelief. What had he done wrong?

His eyebrows knitted together as he glanced over at the stoic Sedrick. "But you know that already. How is that possible? I know Melody and I haven't seen each other that much over the last few months. It's been busy and I've had to cancel trips. I thought she understood." He paused. "I've sent dozens of flowers."

He hesitated again. "Maybe I should have sent gifts. I remember sending a diamond bracelet to a woman I was dating, and she forgave me."

Sedrick narrowed his gaze. "Of course, Melody, and one of your past girlfriends, are exactly the same and therefore she is the kind of person who could be bought."

William flinched, noting the open sarcasm in Sedrick voice. "What is that supposed to mean?"

"You know exactly what it means. Melody is not like the other women you have dated. She and I had many conversations when she visited, and you were occupied with business. She did not care that you have money or a title. She loves you for who you are. A rare thing in your world. She can't be bought. The real question is how do you feel about her? If you do love her the way I suspect you do, Oly is right. You have really mucked things up this time."

"I'll make it right. I know she wants to see more of New Zealand. I'll carve out a few days…"

"You don't have a few days, Sedrick said interrupting. "With respect, sir. You are a fool. Didn't you listen to Oly's message? Or the tone in Melody's voice? She is upset with you. Melody doesn't only want more days with you, she wants a commitment. From the first time Melody visited you in New Zealand, it was obvious that Melody was not the kind of woman a person just dates. She is the kind of woman a person marries."

"And you know I believe that marriage won't work for me. The estate takes too much of my time and you saw what it did to my parent's relationship."

"So, now you are also fortune teller and can foresee the future?" Sedrick said, frowning. "You can't know that marriage with Melody won't work. What you should be asking yourself is if you love her enough to try. Don't use your parent's failed marriage as an excuse. Learn from their mistakes." Sedrick picked up the tea service on the table and frowned. "But if you are hell bent on allowing this breakup, it seems that Melody has done you a great favor by coming here to end the relationship." He lifted an eyebrow. "Shall I inform your exes," Sedrick said with a straight face, "and alert the news media that you are once again available? I believe the Lady Philomena is still single."

William glared at Sedrick. "I don't appreciate your sarcasm. I am not interested in Philomena, nor is she interested in me. We've known each other since we were children and tried to make it work, but it never clicked. I think I read she was planning to marry some rich American oilman a few years ago, or maybe she said the man was the founder of some tech company. I can't remember. But why are we talking about Philomena? You know I'm interested in Melody?"

"I can't believe you're being this dense. According to her message, Melody believes you are not interested and is flying here to break up with you. You will be single again and once news breaks that one of New Zealand's most eligible bachelors is available again, there will be a planeload of egger young women descending on the estate professing their undying love, even though they have never met you. I'll alert the staff to make sure the guest's rooms are prepared."

"You are not helping."

"On the contrary, I believe I'm reminding you of your life before you met Melody. One more thing. The reason I mentioned Philomena is that she arrived while you were away. Oh, and here she is now."

William stood. "She what?"

A tall woman, dressed casually in faded jeans and a powder blue sweater stood in the doorway. She cleared her throat as she tied her blonde hair back in a ponytail. "Good. His royal clueless finally arrived. When do we leave to pick up Melody?"

"What are you doing here?"

"Saving the day." She rolled her eyes. "Obviously." She reached for a biscuit cookie on the tray Sedrick held.

"Would you like tea?"

"That would be lovely, Sedrick. Thank you."

William looked between Philomena and Sedrick as Sedrick set down the tray and poured tea. Odd that he hadn't noticed that there were two teacups and saucers on the tray before. He felt as though Philomena and Sedrick were up to something, but he couldn't tell what it was. He shook away the odd notion. He was being paranoid.

"Melody's plane did not arrive in Auckland as planned," William said. "It landed in Wellington and Oly is driving Melody to the estate. There is no need for us to go anywhere. I repeat. Why are you here?"

She waved away his statement as though it were an annoying fly. "I know that. Sedrick filled me in."

William turned on Sedrick. "Why did you share my messages with Philomena? They were private."

Sedrick shrugged. "A lapse in judgment sir. My apologies."

Philomena finished her biscuit and plopped on the sofa. "You can't be upset with Sedrick. It wasn't his fault. I arrived when he was on the phone, retrieving your messages. The messages were on speaker and I overheard everything."

"Yes, she did," Sedrick said with a slight nod. "Would you like more tea?"

"Stop." William held up his hand. Sedrick never lost his temper and Philomena never visited the estate without notice. The world had turned upside down. It was like the seasons in the northern and southern hemispheres. When it was Fall in one, it was Spring in the other.

"I'm going to take a shower."

"Brilliant idea," Philomena said, reaching for her tea. "Be quick about it, though. We need to leave soon if we plan to arrive at Hobbiton before Oly and Melody."

William's frustration grew. Why wasn't anyone listening to him? "We're not going anywhere. Oly, Amelia and Melody are coming to us. Remember?"

She turned toward Sedrick and heaved a sigh. "Oly and you are so right. William is impossibly dense. Or maybe we've misread the signs after all, and William isn't in love with Melody. That would explain his lack of urgency in running after her when he learned that his gorgeous cousin and his adorable daughter were taking a romantic and leisurely road trip with Melody." She ended her comment with a sly smile and a wink as she sipped her tea. "Nothing to worry about. A woman feeling neglected by her boyfriend meets a handsome and gallant widower. What could possibly go wrong." She winked again. "Or right."

"Oly would never…"

"Of course, not darling. Oly is a gentleman. Which makes him even more attractive to any woman with a pulse. If I thought I had even a smidge of a chance with him I'd wait for him for as long as it took."

"What are you doing here?"

"Isn't it obvious? I'm hoping Oly will give me that chance. Now, hurry up and take your shower. Time is ticking."

CHAPTER SIX

The lush green rolling hills of Hobbiton spread out like a thick carpet. Rows of purple and white snapdragons, framed gardens filled with fragrant white freesia, blue hydrangeas, and blush pink roses. In the distance was the Hobbit Shire, tucked into the hillside as though it had been there for hundreds of years, instead of decades.

Melody yawned and stretched, blinking to make sure she wasn't dreaming. Hobbiton looked so beautiful and serene it didn't seem real. As she buttoned her coat to get ready to get out of the car, Oly headed toward the parking area and Amelia stirred in the backseat.

Melody had expected an amusement park experience. Instead Hobbiton, with its round wood doors tucked into the grassy hills, looked as natural as the trees and flowers surrounding the park-like setting.

Families moved toward the entrance of Hobbiton with child-like expressions of wonder and excitement. She was glad she was here. It was as though the magical atmosphere had melted away her troubles. Even the sun was shining.

Hobbiton, although thousands of miles away from her home in the Northwest, reminded her of the time she'd spent with William at Butchart Gardens in Victoria, Canada over Christmas. At Butchart, the trees and shrubbery had been covered with star-white twinkling lights that shimmered in the moonlight and transported you to a place where anything was possible. It was where she and William had kissed and believed that their relationship would bloom and grow.

When had she stopped believing in them?

She was smart enough to realize that life with someone descended from royalty would not be the way it was in the happily-after fairy tales. But she hadn't expected sustaining a long-distance romance to be as hard as it had been. William had assured her that his family's titles didn't come with the same pomp and circumstance as English royalty. They wouldn't be chased by the Paparazzi and his family didn't have a hidden underground vault that housed diamond tiaras and emerald and ruby necklaces. William considered himself a businessman, not a royal. Hundreds of lives depended on him to make the right decision and he took his responsibilities seriously.

She'd fallen in love with that man and how much he cared about the people entrusted to his care. What had taken her by surprise was the toll those responsibilities had had on their relationship. What it boiled down to was simple. Did she loved William enough to revise her vision of a happily ever after scenario?

"We've arrived at Hobbiton," Oly announced as he parked the car and reached for his cell phone. He pulled up his message from the Hobbiton tour section and typed in a response, then pressed send. "According to the message, the guide will meet us for our personal tour at the entrance. I just let him know we've arrived."

Melody checked her own messages. There were several from her Aunt Casey asking for an update and requesting Melody take lots of pictures. Still no messages from William. Instead of calling, she typed in a quick text, telling him she'd arrived at Hobbiton.

She mentally bounced back and forth in her thoughts between being annoyed that he hadn't responded to her messages and worrying that something might have happened to him. She pulled up the phone number for Sedrick, then changed her mind about calling him. During her visits to William's estate, she and Sedrick had become friends. He had told her about William's adventures as a child and she had confessed that she believed she was falling in love with William.

She knew that if anything had happened to William, Sedrick would have called her.

Melody grabbed her messenger-style purse and slung it across her body as she joined Oly to help Amelia. The curt, and impersonal messages she'd sent to William bothered her. Was she trying to distance herself from him to protect her heart?

She watched as Oly put on Amelia's shoes, all the while talking about the sights they would see today. He was so patient. Relationships weren't cookie-cutter any more than the type of a family dynamic. Neither were a one-size-fits-all scenario these days. When her parents died, she was raised by her aunts and Oly would be raising Amelia as a single parent. It dawned on Melody that the only thing that matter was love and respect.

Her relationship with William wasn't like the majority of matches she and her aunts made. Single people came to the Matchmaker Café, seeking their soulmates. Generally, couples they matched lived in the same city. The aunts shied away from encouraging long distance relationships, reasoning that they were too difficult to maintain. Maybe the aunts were wrong. Wasn't distance just another obstacle to be overcome when two people were truly in love?

"I don't want to wear a coat," Amelia announced with a pout.

"It might rain, and I don't want you getting wet and chilled," Oly said holding out a pink coat with a red rose on the collar.

Amelia looked at the clear sky and narrowed her gaze. "It doesn't look like rain."

Observing the exchange between Oly and Amelia, Melody smiled to herself, fighting down a laugh as her somber mood lifted. Children had that effect on her. She loved their child-like innocence and in this case, Amelia had a point and was winning the argument. There wasn't a cloud in the sky. Another thing she loved was parents who were cautious and protective when it came to their children. She considered that a very good thing.

She lifted her face to the sun, soaking in the gentle rays. It wasn't as warm as the sun would be at this time of year in Seattle and for some reason that was okay. This was New Zealand. William's home. When she arrived at his estate, she planned to talk to William, really talk. Not the, you-better-marry-me-or-else, talk. She wanted the talk where they would be honest with each other as to where they thought their relationship was headed. And if they were on a slow track to finding their happily-ever-after, what was the rush?

The real question was if William loved her as much as she loved him. If that was the case, she could wait.

"Daddy," Amelia said, breaking into Melody's thoughts. "I want to take my teddy bear, Freddie, on the tour with us."

"No worries," Melody said. "I'll get him for you."

Melody climbed into the backseat, moving one of the suitcases out of the way. "I can't find it."

Oly ducked his head to peer into the backseat. "Freddie might have dropped to the floor or between Amelia's car seat and the car door."

Melody scooted toward the car seat. Just as Oly predicted, the teddy bear was wedged between the seat and the door. "Got it." She grabbed Freddie and backed out of the car and into Oly. The contact made her lose her balance but Oly put his arm around her to catch her before she fell.

"Uncle Billy," Amelia squealed, running from Oly toward a tall man and woman who had parked in the parking spot next to Oly's and were getting out of a black pickup truck.

Melody handed the teddy bear to Oly and straightened. "William? What are you doing here?"

William knelt to give Amelia a big hug as the woman presented Amelia with a Hobbit doll. The woman had a blonde ponytail and a white puffy coat that looked more suitable to the slopes than fall weather in New Zealand. Melody didn't recognize the woman, but Amelia seemed to know her.

Amelia gave the woman a hug as William marched in the direction of Melody and Oly. When he stood in front of Oly, his expression darkened. "If I wasn't concerned that Amelia would be concerned that we were fighting," he said, lowering his voice. "I'd punch you in the nose."

"Great to see you too, cousin. But have you lost your mind? What are you talking about?"

William gritted his teeth. "Move away from Melody. Now."

Amelia waved as she held onto Philomena's hand. "Daddy. Philomena gave me a Hobbit doll. Isn't he cute? Can Philomena come with us on the tour?"

"Of course, sweetheart," Oly said, then turned to glower at William. "I don't know what your problem is, but there's nothing going on between Melody and me. Now, if you'll excuse me, my daughter wants to see the Hobbit Shire." He turned toward Melody. "Don't let him give you any crap."

"What's that supposed to mean?" William said.

"Wait," Melody said. "You two know each other?"

"I'll let William explain," Oly said.

She should be hopping mad. Oly knew William They were cousins. And who was Philomena? She would confront Oly later. Right now, there was a more immediate problem to deal with. Why was William here and why was he acting so strange?

Melody waited until Oly, Amelia and Philomena, were far enough away so that she wouldn't be overheard and then turned to face William. "Oly is right," she said, trying to keep her frustration under control. "What is your problem? Do you think something is going on between Oly and me? How dare you. He just gave me a ride. A ride to see you, I might add. I've been sending you messages since my plane landed didn't you receive them?"

"Oly left me a message that you wanted to break up with me." His voice was flat and lifeless.

At that moment she wished she was a mind reader. William was giving off conflicting emotions. When he first arrived, he had seemed jealous of Oly. Now she couldn't read him. Was he resigned that she wanted to break up with him, or did he seem sad?

She crossed her arms, eyeing the man standing before her. He was dressed casually in jeans and a faded, flannel plaid shirt. In all the times they'd spent together, he'd worn suits or designer slacks and sweaters.

"For the moment I'll ignore that Oly didn't tell me you two were related or that he sent you the message. The bigger issue on my mind," she said pressing her lips together, "is you thought because I planned to break up with you, I'd make a pass at the first man I saw. Typical male behavior. You are a bloody Neanderthal. I'm going on the tour with Oly and Amelia."

William stepped in front of her to block her path. "Melody. Please don't go."

His words when straight to her heart and warmed her to her core. He loved her. She didn't need to hear the words. They were in his voice and the way his eyes searched hers.

She hugged her arms closer, knowing he wasn't talking about the tour. She knew he was asking her to give him another chance. She'd never seen him like this before. It wasn't just that he was jealous, or dressed differently, he looked like a different person. He looked approachable and vulnerable. She liked this William. He seemed like someone who she could talk to; someone who would listen.

He stuffed his hands in his pockets. "I've been a jerk. I've allowed everything to come between us and when I listened to your messages and then saw you with Oly and something broke inside me. I'm worried that I've lost you."

She heard the pain in his voice. She squeezed her eyes shut, remembering all the times she'd used the Matchmaker Café on Lake Union as an excuse for not returning his calls right away. If she was being honest, she was trying to pay him back for not answering her calls as fast as she would have liked. There was blame to go around on both sides. "It takes two to make a relationship work and I'm just as guilty. I was afraid. What if it doesn't work?"

He took her hands in his. "What if it does?"

"It's scary."

"Does that mean you're giving me a second chance?"

Her eyes blurred with happy tears as she moved closer to him and nodded. "I'm hoping we both deserve a second chance."

He tucked a strand of hair behind her ear. "You know what was scarier for me? Seeing you with Oly's arm around you. I knew in that moment that I could lose you and it was like the ground disappeared beneath my feet. I felt lost and off balance. I knew in that instant I was in love with you. That you were the most important person in my life. Please give me another chance."

The sun shone brighter as she moved into his arms. "I love you too."

His lips covered hers like the breath of a spring sun, with the promise of warm days and nights filled with stars. The kiss deepened, chasing away doubt and pain.

"Will you marry me," he said against her lips.

"Yes," she promised.

The End

BIO

Pam Binder is a USA Today and New York Times bestselling author, conference speaker, and the president of the Pacific Northwest Writers Association. Pam writes romance, time travel, fantasy and young adult fiction. She loves writing Christmas stories, and her newest Christmas romance, *Gingerbread Knight*, will be released in the fall of 2021.

Made in the USA
Middletown, DE
04 October 2021